Ruthann

Brides of Fremont County, Book 3

by Cat Cahill

D1736921

Copyright

Chapter One

CAÑON CITY, COLORADO – June 1881

Ruthann Joliet had run out of suitors—again.

She sighed as she watched her latest beau move quickly down the street. Foster Jones had been none too happy when she told him she thought it best they remain as friends. She lifted her forehead from the window and moved to the settee, where the man's full cup of tea still rested on a silver serving platter on the nearby table.

It wasn't as if she didn't care for Mr. Jones. In fact, she thought him quite witty and reasonably handsome. Any other girl would have been thrilled that he'd chosen to court her. And Ruthann was too, at first.

She lifted her own cup of tea and took a sip of the now-tepid liquid. After six different suitors, she'd hoped Mr. Jones might be the one to make her heart beat a little faster, to make her long for his return when he left, to be the face that appeared in her dreams at night. But try as she might, none of that had happened.

As mad as he was about her ending the courtship, he must have already known what was in her mind. Their conversations had been restrained and stiff. He hadn't even asked her to call him Foster.

"Ruthann?"

She looked up to see her dearest friend, Norah Parker in the doorway. Norah's red hair sat in a low chignon with a few prettily arranged curls left loose, and her big blue eyes narrowed as she took in Ruthann's somber state. She came immediately to the settee and reached for Ruthann's hand.

"Mr. Jones?" she asked.

Ruthann nodded. "How did you know?"

"I saw him stomping away from here, looking as if he were spoiling for a fight."

Ruthann grimaced. She hoped Mr. Jones simply went home, rather than getting himself into trouble. "He took it so badly."

"Rejection isn't something most people take lightly," Norah said in her soft voice. She squeezed Ruthann's hand. "But you did the right thing. It was better to send him along than to let this drag on. Or to wake up one day and find yourself unhappily married."

"I doubt I'll ever find myself married at all."

"Nonsense. The right man will come along."

Ruthann forced herself to smile at Norah. She knew Norah meant every word she said, but after having found six suitors wanting, Ruthann wasn't so certain anymore.

And it wasn't as if the men who had courted her were hideous or cruel or cold. On the contrary, they'd all been perfectly decent, just like Mr. Jones. She'd thought each one of them had the potential to make her happy. Yet each time, there had been something missing.

Ruthann couldn't see herself falling in love with any of them.

"I suppose if the right man doesn't come along, I can be that kindly spinster daughter who cares for her parents in their old age," Ruthann said with a shrug.

Norah eyed her for a moment, and then they both collapsed in laughter.

"Can you imagine?" Norah asked, her face lit in amusement.

"Oh, I can. They'll still be trying to find the right man for me. I'll be sixty years of age and they'll have invited some widower over for supper." Ruthann smiled at the thought. It was fun to laugh about now, but not something she particularly wished to endure in her older years.

"Perhaps Stuart will take pity upon you and let you live with him and his future wife," Norah said.

Ruthann leveled a gaze at her friend.

"Or perhaps not." Norah's lips twitched as if she were trying hard not to laugh.

"I'd much rather live by myself in some cottage at the edge of town than listen to my brother telling me what to do when I'm well past the age to be told." Ruthann paused. "Besides, he has yet to show interest in marriage. At this point, we'll both wind up old and alone. And he'll still likely have words with any fellow I might find the slightest bit charming."

Norah looked somewhere over Ruthann's shoulder, her face taking on a neutral expression and her eyes far away.

Ruthann's heart pinched as she thought back over her words. "I'm sorry," she said as she laid a hand on Norah's arm.

Norah's gaze found her again, and her lips lifted into the ghost of a smile. "It's all right. You did nothing wrong. I've just had Jeremy on my mind lately."

Ruthann nodded as her mind counted back the months. It had been one year since Norah had effectively lost her brother. He was still very much alive, but he might as well be counted among the dead considering she wouldn't see him again for thirty years.

"Have your parents relented? Can you visit him?" Ruthann asked. It was a shame to know that Jeremy was so nearby, and yet Norah was forbidden from seeing him.

Norah shook her head. "They're too ashamed. They prefer to pretend he *is* dead. And if I went to that prison . . ." She shuddered. "They'd likely think the same of me."

"I very much doubt that," Ruthann said. "They would be angry, but they'd forgive you."

Norah pressed her lips together, and Ruthann had the distinct feeling there was something more behind Norah's decision to follow her parents' wishes. Ruthann's heart ached for her friend. She couldn't imagine having Stuart accused of some terrible crime and sent off to the State Penitentiary—the prison just past the edge of town that everyone still called the Territorial Prison—for most of his life.

"Tell me," she said, trying to lift Norah's spirits. "Has Mr. Beck sent you any gifts lately?"

Norah giggled. "Dear old Mr. Beck. He sent me a chicken yesterday. A chicken! Who sends a lady a chicken?"

"Well, he certainly is practical," Ruthann said.

"That he is. A chicken, a bottle of fresh milk, a broom." Norah counted the odd gifts on her fingers. "I fear he might send a hog next!"

"A hog would mean he's truly smitten," Ruthann teased.

"I've tried to tell him—more than once—that I don't wish for his attentions. Yet, he continues to send me gifts. Perhaps I've been too gentle? I don't want to injure his pride."

"Whose pride are you ladies injuring?" Stuart, Ruthann's older brother entered the room, pressing himself into the conversation. He glanced around. "What happened to Foster?"

"I don't believe Mr. Jones will be returning," Ruthann said as lightly as she could muster. "Unlike Norah's Mr. Beck, who is most persistent."

Stuart furrowed his brow as he took a seat in the wing chair opposite them. "Beck is my father's age."

"Precisely," Norah said.

"And if you've sent Foster away, I say good riddance," Stuart said to Ruthann. "I dislike the way he always arrives earlier than he says he will."

Ruthann gave her brother a sidelong glance. "There isn't a thing wrong with Mr. Jones, and you know it. He'll make some woman very happy—just not me."

"I doubt that. You've made a wise decision," Stuart said, clearly not willing to let Ruthann have the last word, as usual.

Ruthann made a face at Norah, who covered her mouth with a gloved hand to hide a smile. If it were up to Stuart, no man would ever measure up. Although Ruthann had begun to wonder the same about her own opinions.

All she wanted was to feel *love*. To have her heart pound uncontrollably when she looked at a man, to wish he might take her in his arms, to lose herself in daydreams of a long life together. Sometimes she wondered if she were asking for too much.

"How was the freight office today?" Norah asked Stuart, and Ruthann could have hugged her for changing the subject away from beaux and courting.

"Busy. I doubt we'll see Papa before dusk. He hasn't touched the books yet today—and you know he won't let me help with them." Stuart ran a hand through his tousled dark blond hair, the exact shade of Ruthann's own. Their eyes were the same color of blue, they sported the same slightly upturned nose, and even their smiles matched. Ruthann couldn't have denied he was her brother if she'd wanted—no one would have believed her.

"I'm happy he's busy." Ruthann kept the last part of her thoughts to herself. If Papa was too busy with the business, he wouldn't have time to scheme with Mama to place a new potential beau in Ruthann's path. "Will you bring lunch back to him? Mama and I set some aside for you both."

Stuart nodded and stood. "I'm famished." He took a few steps toward the door before stopping and turning back around. "I almost forgot! Who do you suppose came into the office this morning?"

Ruthann looked to Norah, who shrugged.

"Nate Harper. Do you remember him?" Stuart asked.

Ruthann's heart skipped a beat. Remember Nate Harper, her brother's closest friend? How could she have ever *forgotten*? "Yes," she managed to say in an even, although breathy, voice. "He . . . he left to join the Army, if I remember correctly." Of course she remembered correctly. She remembered everything about Nate.

Stuart nodded. "He did. Joined the cavalry in fact, and now he's back home. And found a place in town to start a business. Photography." He shook his head as if he couldn't imagine Nate Harper operating a photographic camera. "After all these years, I thought he'd gone for good."

"As did I," Ruthann said in a strangled voice.

Stuart looked at her a moment, and Ruthann feared he knew exactly what went through her mind. But then he smiled, and bade them good afternoon before retreating to the kitchen.

The second he was gone, Norah grabbed Ruthann's hand. "Nathaniel Harper. He . . . he . . ."

"Kissed me and left town," Ruthann finished for her.

Nate was the reason no beau of Ruthann's ever measured up to the standards in her head.

And now he'd returned.

Chapter Two

THE SIGN WAS SIMPLE and unimpressive, but it conveyed the information needed to passersby:

Harper Photographic Studio

Nathaniel Harper stood back and locked his hands behind him. It would do for the time being, he figured, until he'd found enough business to warrant purchasing a more professional sign. Even as he stood assessing how it looked above the door, more than one passing townsperson eyed the sign with curiosity. That was reassuring. He was not the only photographer in town, but with the way Cañon City was growing, he hoped there would be plenty of customers eager for a photograph.

And growing it was. Nate hardly recognized the Cañon City he'd left six years ago. Here and there, a few places remained the same. A church, the sheriff's office and jail, Mrs. Smith's restaurant, the dusty roads, Murray's Saloon, the McClure House hotel. But those familiar places were vastly outnumbered by the construction of newer buildings and the sheer quantity of people Nate passed on the streets.

Happy enough with the sign, Nate returned to the interior of the building he'd rented from a man eager to have a tenant. It wasn't much to look at inside yet. He'd set up a makeshift studio space, with a settee, some drapes, and an end table he'd found in the mess upstairs. The fellow who'd rented this space before had lived on the second floor—and it looked as if he hadn't taken a thing with him from that space when he left.

Nate leaned against the wall and assessed the space before him. He needed a few chairs to swap out with the settee and some decorative items for the end table. A candelabra wouldn't go amiss, nor would a fancy lamp. The more options he had to work with, the happier the people who came for photos would be.

With what he had, though, he was ready to open the doors to customers. The darkroom was prepared in the rear of the building in what used to be a storeroom, and he'd brought all of his equipment, plates, and chemicals with him. He had enough to last a couple of months, provided business was steady. It wouldn't be too difficult to order more from Denver.

His camera sat ready on the tripod he'd bought off a surveyor a few years ago. He rested a hand on the camera, remembering the joy he'd felt upon purchasing it. Photography had been the only thing that had lightened the darkness he'd slipped into after the Great Sioux War years ago. It had been the only thing that made him rise in the morning, and the only way he could distract himself from the vivid memories that would otherwise haunt him at night.

Nate dropped his hand. Those days were behind him now. And hopefully, with returning home to Cañon City, he could finally leave behind the memories he'd rather forget, and become the man he used to be.

But right now, it was time to get this business off the ground, which meant opening the door to potential customers.

And so he did just that, striding to the front door, opening it, and propping it with a small stone. He stood out front a moment, basking in the warmth of the sun and taking in the sights around him. Scrubby hills rose outside of town, with shadowy blue mountains not far behind them to the south and west. If it were silent, perhaps he could have heard the rushing of the Arkansas River, but it wasn't quiet at all here on Main Street. People strode the plank sidewalks, and horses and wagons clattered down the dirt road. The clanging hammer in a blacksmith's shop ricocheted against the nearby buildings.

Nate closed his eyes and took in the sounds and the scent of the air. As much as it had changed, it was good to be home. It sounded normal here. It was a place where bad memories could most certainly disappear, never to be experienced again.

"Pardon me, sir?" A feminine voice interrupted Nate's reverie.

His eyes flew open to find a petite young woman with dark hair and a pointed chin standing across from him. She was dressed in yellow ruffles with a parasol to match. He didn't recognize her from his life here before. Her eyes narrowed and widened within the span of a moment, as if she'd suddenly changed her mind about him.

"Yes?" he asked. Something about the set of her jaw and the way she looked at him made him wary. He wanted to brush it off as ridiculous, but too many years spent waiting for foes to approach had honed Nate's senses.

"Are you the photographer?" She gestured at his sign.

"I am." He ought to ask her if she was in need of a photograph. He could certainly use the business after all, but that earlier intuition kept him silent.

"Oh, how wonderful!" The girl's face changed entirely, from something calculating to downright gushing. She pressed the hand that didn't hold the parasol to her chest. "Could you take my photograph?"

No. Nate pushed the thought away. He'd be foolish to turn down his first customer. But maybe . . . He glanced inside his studio. He should take a few test photographs first, to ensure everything was set up properly. It wouldn't do to hand a paying customer a photograph that needed more light or had items nearby that cast unflattering shadows.

"Yes," he made himself say. "Could you come back tomorrow? I've only just set up."

The young woman's cheerful expression dropped into a frown for a fraction of a second before she smiled again and held out her gloved hand. "I will. Thank you, Mr. . . .?"

Nate looked down at her hand, knowing what was expected. Ignoring the wariness that crept up his spine, he took her hand briefly in his and inclined his head. "Nathaniel Harper." He dropped her hand as quickly as propriety would allow.

"I am Miss Flagler," she said, clutching that parasol with both hands. "I'll look forward to seeing you tomorrow." She held his gaze for longer than was necessary, and when she finally drew her eyes from him to make her way down the road, Nate was left with such a disconcerting feeling that it seemed he couldn't breathe properly. He tugged at his collar, eying Miss Flagler as she walked away.

He couldn't place a finger on what it was about her that had set him so on edge, but the feeling was too strong to be ignored. She'd said nothing unusual or troublesome. Besides being perhaps a bit too forward, she'd taken no actions that should arouse such a feeling.

Was he being too sensitive? Cañon City was not the cavalry, and the people here were not his enemies, waiting for him to let down his guard so they could jump in for the kill.

Perhaps it had simply been too long since he'd had a normal conversation with a woman.

At any rate, she would likely be his first paying customer, and for that, he should be thankful. Now, to find someone willing to sit in for a test of his camera. Nate took off his hat and ran a hand over his hair before replacing it. Jasper Hill and his mother, who ran the general store, were far too busy, judging from the constant stream of people walking through the doors. The minister at the nearby church might be an option. Maybe Nate could offer the test photograph as a gift, and invite the man to bring his wife and children.

Mind made up, he closed the door to his studio and crossed the street. The church was only a block down, on Macon Street, but a scene in front of the hardware store made him stop in his tracks.

A young woman wearing a simple blue gown stood pressed against the wall of the building, and a man several decades her senior towered over her.

Nate squinted at them. The man was clearly upset about something. He had a finger raised and was shaking it at the lady. And she . . . Nate drew in a breath. *It couldn't be.* He wasn't ready to see her again.

And yet it *was* her. Dark blonde hair, as soft as silk, was drawn up under a straw bonnet, and a sweet round face looked up at the man in front of her. He couldn't see her eyes from this distance, but he'd never forget them. They were the clearest blue, the sky on a sunny July day. And those pink lips . . .

His breath shuddered through him as he pushed *that* memory away too. It was Ruthann Joliet, Stuart's little sister. Except now she was all grown up. And—apparently—facing down a monster of a man.

Some protective instinct roiled through Nate, and he clenched his hands into fists at his sides. Without thinking, he took decisive steps forward toward the pair.

He didn't know what he was going to do, but he knew one thing for certain: no one would hurt Ruthann Joliet while he was around to stop it.

Chapter Three

RUTHANN CLUTCHED HER reticule as poor Mr. McGregor took another step toward her. He was uncomfortably close, but that wasn't out of the ordinary.

"I *told* him, Miss Ruthann, I *told* him—"

Out of nowhere, a man grabbed hold of Mr. McGregor's arm and turned him squarely around so that he was facing away from Ruthann. Mr. McGregor stumbled a little, but the hand wrapped around his arm held him tight.

"You need to back away from the lady." The voice connected to the hand that held on to Mr. McGregor sounded low but familiar.

Ruthann's heart thumped, and she pushed herself out from behind Mr. McGregor. There, holding fast to the man the entire town tended to look after, stood Nate Harper. He was older, his jaw more angled, his dark hair shorter, his shoulders broader, but Ruthann would recognize him anywhere. And when he turned those brown eyes toward Ruthann, her breath caught in her throat.

He looked her up and down, and something in his face flickered. Ruthann's heart fairly yearned to see him smile at her, but instead he kept his hardened expression in place and said, "Miss Joliet, is this fellow bothering you?"

Miss Joliet? The formality of it all sent a giggle up Ruthann's throat, which she strangled with a cough. "He is not," she finally managed to say. "And I'll thank you to let the poor man's arm go. Mr. McGregor was merely telling me about the new shipment of pencils that arrived at the general store. He does love his pencils. Mr. McGregor, this is Nate Harper. Nate, this is Finnegan McGregor." She gave Mr. McGregor an encouraging smile.

That seemed to lift his spirits, and once again, he began animatedly talking about his collection of pencils and how he might purchase another to add to it. The expression on Nate's face relaxed as it became clear he realized Mr. McGregor was hardly a threat to an insect, much less a woman. He let the man's arm go and politely listened to his ramblings.

"Perhaps," Ruthann said in the space it took Mr. McGregor to take a breath, "we ought to walk home with you? I imagine Sarah is beginning to worry."

"Oh, yes. Yes, that would be nice," Mr. McGregor said, his usual smile still upon his face.

That decided, Ruthann looped an arm around the older man's elbow. "Would you like to come?" she asked Nate.

He looked across the road at something, and then quickly back to her and nodded, still as stoic as he was before. And as they began walking—and Mr. McGregor began speaking again, this time about his sister Sarah's homemade biscuits—Ruthann found her eyes drifting back toward Nate.

When had he become so serious? The boy who had stolen a kiss from her before he'd left town had been lighthearted and jovial. He'd been as quick with a teasing quip as with a smile. He was no longer a boy, that was for certain, but it looked as if his entire personality had changed too. And there was something about his eyes, something dark and faraway and somewhat sad.

Nate walked quietly alongside them, murmured a polite greeting to Sarah McGregor when they delivered her brother safely home at the edge of town, and then said nothing as they began the walk back into town.

If there was to be conversation, it appeared as if the responsibility for it lay with Ruthann. And she *so* desperately wanted conversation with Nate Harper.

"It's good to have you back home, Nate." She refused to call him *Mr. Harper*.

He gave a quick nod. "It was time."

What did that mean? Feeling as if it were rude to pry, Ruthann searched for another topic. "My brother said you were starting a photography business. Is that true?"

"It is." He looked resolutely ahead.

"How fascinating. How did you learn to operate a photograph camera?"

"In the Army." He paused, as if he were considering whether to elaborate. "A fellow working for a publication back East came to take photographs of the Great Western Army, as he put it. He was especially enamored with the cavalry." The ghost of a smile lifted Nate's lips, and for a second, Ruthann saw the boy she knew.

"He stayed for nearly a year, following us around and setting up his camera. I found the equipment and the process fascinating, and he was kind enough to show me how it all worked. Before he left, I'd ordered myself a camera. The officers humored me, especially because it made the men happy to have photographs to send home. I'd even set up a makeshift dark-room."

"How interesting! And now you've decided to go into busi-ness with it?" Ruthann had a million other questions, none of which she dared ask. For instance, why hadn't he written them in all those years? Hadn't he missed her brother? Hadn't he missed *her*?

"I have." Nate had grown quiet again, as if he'd used up his allotted words when he'd spoken of learning about photogra-phy.

Pushing the urgent, yet embarrassing questions in her mind away, Ruthann asked, "What of your horse?" She'd loved Apollo, a sleek chestnut gelding Nate had saved every hard-earned penny for when they were young.

"He died some years ago." Nate's expression didn't change, and he didn't offer any further explanation.

Ruthann pressed her lips together, hoping she hadn't caused him any distress. And yet . . . he was making conversa-tion so very difficult. It oughtn't be left up to one person to car-ry the weight of the conversation, and yet here she was, trying to think of another question. It made a girl wonder if the fellow next to her had any interest in conversing at all.

"What—" she said at the exact moment he said, "How—"

Ruthann laughed, simply grateful he was interested enough to pose a question to her. "Please, you speak first."

His eyes lightened some as he looked at her, as if their blun-der had pushed away the cloud that had settled over him. "All right. Stuart said your parents were doing well. How is your friend, Miss Parker? And her brothers?"

Ruthann hated to be the one to bear bad news. Norah's brothers, Jeremy and Charles, had been good friends of Nate and Stuart's. "Norah is well, as is Charles. He married recently—to Mary Evans, who you may recall."

"Oh, yes." Nate's eyebrows lifted in amusement, and Ruthann bit back a smile. Mary had pined after Charles for years, and he'd finally taken notice.

"Jeremy . . ." There was no kind way to put it. "He's in the Territorial Prison for robbery and murder." When Nate glanced down at her in surprise, Ruthann added, "None of us believe he was guilty, of course. But the judge thought otherwise."

Nate shook his head. He was quiet for a moment as they passed the new schoolhouse. It was larger than the one where they'd all attended school together—some more often than others. Ruthann distinctly remembered Nate and Stuart sneaking off on occasion in the mornings, sometimes with Jeremy or Charles. She'd often watched them go, wishing she could tag along.

As they approached the center of town, Ruthann wondered if Nate was planning to walk her all the way home. Her heart soared at the thought. With each step, her hopes grew a little more.

Until Nate paused just before the hardware store where she'd met him earlier. As her heart was about to plummet, he spoke.

"I wondered—that is, well . . ." He glanced across the road, and Ruthann followed his gaze to a building with a hand-painted sign sitting just above the door. *Harper Photographic Studio.*

Nate straightened and looked back at her, his jaw carefully set as if he didn't want to convey any emotion whatsoever. He likely didn't realize that it gave a pensive look to the sharp angles of his face, where the beginnings of a beard were just beginning to show along his cheeks and chin. Ruthann wondered if it would feel rough beneath her fingers.

Her eyes widened at the thought and she quickly looked away in fear he would know exactly what she was thinking. Her face burned, and she pretended to search for something in her reticule until the heat dissipated from her own cheeks.

"I need to test my equipment," he finally said. "It would be easier with a subject. Would you mind . . . I mean, would you be interested in sitting for a few photographs?"

Ruthann looked up in surprise. He was asking her to spend more time with him?

"Of course, we would have the front door open. You needn't fear gossip," he said.

She was so caught up in the idea that Nate wanted to spend more time with her that the thought of impropriety hadn't even crossed her mind.

"It's quite all right," he said quickly. "You don't have—"

"Yes! Yes, I would love to help you out," Ruthann said as quickly as possible.

Nate's neutral expression brightened. Had she made him happy? She hoped so.

"Thank you," was all he said.

And then she followed the man she'd loved since she was thirteen years old across the road to his studio.

Chapter Four

THE FOLLOWING MORNING dawned bright and clear with a lingering chill in the air, but Nate hardly felt it as he walked from his boardinghouse to the photography studio. He'd been awake since the first hint of light in the sky, eager to get back to his work.

Ruthann Joliet had been the ideal test subject, sitting perfectly still for the fifteen minutes it took for the exposure of her image onto the plate. In between photographs, she'd kept up a lively chatter, asking him about the camera and the process of developing the plates along with filling him in on various people he'd known in town years ago. She didn't inquire about his time in the Army, much to Nate's relief.

It had been the most enjoyable afternoon he'd spent in a very long time.

He'd only developed two of the plates last night before returning to the boardinghouse, and looking at the images now made him smile. Ruthann. He knew he shouldn't think of her as *Ruthann*. After all, she was a grown woman now, not the little sister who followed Stuart around when they were younger. And far too many years had passed since he'd acted on his raging desire to kiss her.

Yet she insisted upon calling him Nate, and he'd caught a sidelong look of exasperation when he referred to her as Miss

Joliet in the studio. But he didn't dare let that wall of propriety down, especially when he could hardly look away from her sweet smile and the way her hair caught the sunlight that had streamed in through the window and open door. He'd always thought her pretty when they were young, but the word wasn't enough for what Ruthann had grown into.

She was, quite simply, beautiful.

And more than that, she still had a tender heart. He certainly hadn't expected to find himself accompanying her to ensure a man like Mr. McGregor returned to his home unscathed. But Ruthann had always been like that, looking out for those who needed help.

He'd stared at the finished photograph far too long, admiring the face that looked back at him instead of assessing the quality of the image. He set it down and ran a hand over his face before picking it up again.

After adjusting the angle of the scene he'd created in order to catch more of the sunlight, he retreated to the darkroom again to develop more of the plates he'd taken yesterday. Ruthann's lovely face looked up at him again and again, and he found himself pausing to bask in it, his thoughts everywhere and nowhere at once.

When a knock came at the door, he jumped, his mind going straight to Stuart. Guilt flooded through him, the same as it had six years ago. His friend would never forgive him for what he'd done, if he knew. Ruthann was out of Nate's reach. Far, far out of his reach, as she should be. He never should have invited her to sit for photographs yesterday. Stuart was probably furious with him.

Setting the last plate down, Nate opened the darkroom door. But the person waiting on the other side wasn't Stuart after all.

It was the petite, dark-haired woman he'd met outside the building yesterday.

"Good morning," he said formally, his hands wrapped around the edges of his jacket.

"Good morning, Mr. Harper," she said, her smile as wide as her eyes.

He glanced behind her—she wasn't alone, thankfully. An older woman, slender and nearly as tall as Nate himself, waited near the front door.

The instant worry that had appeared with the younger woman's presence dissipated. "Are you here for photographs?"

"I am! How did you know?" She giggled behind a hand and Nate fought the urge to sigh. This was not going to be his most enjoyable session.

But his business wouldn't survive without actual customers, and if this girl wanted photographs, he would take them without complaint.

Nate gestured at the settee and end table set up in front of the drapes. The woman put her reticule down and made her way to the settee.

"You may go now," she said somewhat coldly to the older lady at the door.

"But Miss Flagler—"

The look Miss Flagler gave the woman could have melted steel, and before Nate could protest, the woman was gone.

He glanced at Miss Flagler, now arranging her skirts just so. She gave him a coquettish smile, and Nate's stomach turned.

He went to the door and opened it, just as he had for Ruthann's session yesterday.

Miss Flagler laughed, as if she found his actions amusing, and every hair on the back of Nate's neck stood up.

"I'm ready for my photograph," she said.

Nate still stood near the door. He could end this right now—show her out immediately. And then . . . what? If he angered her, she could spread the word that he'd refused her business. Judging from the fine clothing and jewelry she wore, Miss Flagler's family likely held some sway in town.

And so he drew in a deep breath and pushed the instinctive worry out of his mind as he crossed back to his camera. He instructed her to remain perfectly still as he took the first image. Unlike with Ruthann yesterday, when the fifteen minutes for the exposure passed in companionable silence, the minutes now dragged out until they felt like hours.

With the first exposure finally finished, Miss Flagler requested a photograph of her standing.

"It's better to see my dress, after all," she said, giving him what most men might see as a disarming smile. But it only made Nate grow more tense, especially with the way she watched him as he moved away from the camera.

He paused a good three feet away from her and directed her to stand at an angle that would best capture the light. When she was arranged just so, he returned to the camera to change the plate and begin the process of taking another photograph. The time stretched on again, and he found himself hoping she wouldn't request a third image.

"This is wonderful fun, isn't it?" she said when Nate indicated she could move again. She retrieved a fan from where it hung at her waist and began to fan herself.

"Indeed," Nate said noncommittally. The room *was* growing warm, but he wasn't certain whether that was from the temperature outside or Nate's growing discomfort with Miss Flagler.

"May I have one more image?" she asked, dipping her head to look up at him through her eyelashes.

"Certainly," Nate forced himself to say. One more, and then it would be over with. Miss Flagler would be gone and he could go back to . . . to what? Thinking of Ruthann? That was something best left alone. Although with Ruthann on his mind, the memories he'd rather not think of felt much further away.

"I thought perhaps I could . . ." Miss Flagler proceeded to turn the settee before draping herself over it in an awkward sort of lounging position.

"Miss Flagler, I don't think that will . . . The light will cast unflattering shadows," Nate finally said.

"Oh?" She twisted some and rearranged her skirts before frowning. "I'm not sure what to do. Will you help me?" When he didn't answer, she added, "Find the right way to sit. Or stand, perhaps?" She held out a hand, and Nate stared at it.

If Miss Flagler thought he was taking her hand, she was sorely mistaken. Instead, he stepped around the camera and assessed the scene in front of him. "It would look best if you sat up straight and angled yourself toward the front of the building."

"Like this?" Miss Flagler flounced upon the settee and twisted herself sideways.

"Yes, but bring your entire body around."

"Oh!" She giggled, and tried to pull her legs around to face the same direction. "I believe my skirts are caught." She looked down at the floor and then up at Nate with the falsest look of helplessness he had ever seen. "Could you help me? Please?"

It was clear this would never end if he left it up to her. Barely keeping his irritation hidden, he strode to the settee where he proceeded to unwrap the hem of her dress from around the piece of furniture's leg.

"There," he said as he stood—only to have her grab on to his arm and stand up herself.

"Thank you, Mr. Harper," she said in a breathless voice as her fingers dug into his arm and she slid closer to him. "I don't know what I would have done without you." She tilted her head back and parted her lips—and Nate finally shook off the shock of the moment.

He stepped firmly backward and pried her hand from his arm. "I'm sorry, Miss Flagler. I forgot that I have an appointment, and I must cut our session short. I'll have your photographs ready tomorrow, if you'd like to return then."

He barely caught her expression of righteous indignation before turning to collect the plates that needed to be developed.

"Thank you for coming to my studio," he said stiffly before he retreated to the rear, leaving Miss Flagler red-faced and clearly angry.

A moment later, safe in the darkroom, Nate heard the front door close and he let out a breath of relief. Miss Flagler was just as wily as he'd feared she might be when he first met her. He'd met a forward woman more than once, but never one as well-to-do as Miss Flagler.

Nate shuddered at the thought of the man who fell for her flirtations. He doubted Miss Flagler's father would be so understanding if he found out. And that certainly wouldn't end well, particularly if the man was like Nate—far from wealthy.

A man like that would find himself out of business and run out of town.

Chapter Five

THE PARKERS' PARLOR was small yet cozy. Norah's mother had let Ruthann in before apologizing that she had to run to meet a friend for tea. But the blessing of being longtime friends meant it was nothing at all for Ruthann to simply wait in the parlor for Norah's return, which Mrs. Parker had said shouldn't be too long.

It was all quite fine by Ruthann, who basked in the quiet of the Parkers' home with no one else around. Her own house had been busy and loud by comparison this morning, with both her parents and Stuart at home. And the day before, Mama had invited several ladies from church over for sewing. There had hardly been a moment for Ruthann to reflect on the events that had happened two days ago.

But here in the quiet of Norah's home, Ruthann's thoughts wandered immediately to where they'd left off as she'd laid in bed the night before. Nate Harper was even more handsome than he'd been six years ago with that dark hair, the ghost of a beard gracing his chin, and the hard work of a soldier evident in the broadness of his shoulders.

It was hopeless mooning over him like some lovesick girl, and yet that's exactly what Ruthann found herself doing. Despite the fact that the carefree boy she'd known had been replaced by a much more serious man, her heart still beat uncontrollably at the thought of him, and she couldn't stop running every word he'd said to her through her head, over and over.

And then, of course, she relived that one single kiss for approximately the millionth time in her life.

Ruthann stood and walked around Norah's parlor. A handful of photographs graced the mantel over the fireplace. Noticeably gone were the single photo of Jeremy and the family photo that had held the images of all five members of the Parker family. Ruthann ran a finger over the image of Norah, which had been taken upon her sixteenth birthday.

Norah was the only person who knew of that fleeting moment between Ruthann and Nate. It had happened so quickly, and then he'd departed for the Dakota Territory the very next day. She hadn't seen or heard from him since—until two days ago.

He was so stoic, so very composed. It was almost as if he were keeping something inside that he didn't dare let out. But it lingered in his eyes. She'd caught it more than once during the photography session. Ruthann suspected it had something to do with his time in the cavalry, and she yearned to know what it was. But it wasn't her place to ask, and she doubted Nate would tell her if she did. In fact, the simple act of asking might cause him to withdraw from her altogether.

And she didn't know if she could withstand that sort of rejection.

She did, at least, have an excuse to visit him again if she wanted to see the photographs he'd taken. She hadn't mentioned the test session to Stuart. It was entirely innocent, and something one would do to help a friend . . . and yet, she didn't imagine her brother seeing it that way at all. Besides, it felt nice to keep that time she'd passed amiably with Nate to herself. She didn't necessarily want to share it with anyone.

Although, Ruthann surmised, she doubted Nate would keep it secret, and so she might as well speak of it. But for now, in the comfort of her friend's parlor, she would relive the moments alone one last time.

A few minutes passed before Ruthann heard footsteps on the front steps. She hurried to the front door to meet Norah, who was burdened down with a large package.

Ruthann held out her arms to take it, and Norah gratefully handed it over.

"It's a cake," Norah said as she peeled off her gloves. "I went to visit Mrs. Bonner to see how she was getting on since losing her husband, and it seems she's been filling her time with baking."

"Well, I suppose that's good." Ruthann preferred to be busy herself. She'd likely be doing something similar in Mrs. Bonner's position.

She handed the cake back to Norah and followed her to the Parkers' kitchen. The cake turned out to be a lovely sponge cake with a shiny glaze. Norah cut them each a slice and put on some tea. As her friend chatted on and on about Mrs. Bonner, Ruthann had the distinct feeling that Norah was anxious about something.

Even after she poured the tea and sat slices of cake on the table, Norah stood nearby, clutching her hands in front of her.

Ruthann waited a moment for Norah to sit, and when she didn't, Ruthann nodded at the empty chair. Norah perched on the edge of it, ignoring her cake and tea.

"Norah." Ruthann sat back, her own cake forgotten. "Something is clearly troubling you. What is it?"

Her friend shot her a worried look, and Ruthann's mind went ten different places at once. Was it Stuart? A friend? One of Norah's brothers? Ruthann stood and moved to the chair closer to Norah. "Please, what's worrying you so?"

Norah pressed her lips together before speaking, tension edging the face that Ruthann knew so well. "It's Mr. Harper. Nate."

"Is he all right? I saw him only two days ago."

Norah raised her eyebrows, but didn't ask Ruthann's meaning. Instead, to Ruthann's relief, she plunged ahead.

"It's gossip, but while I disbelieve the cause, I fear the result may be true." Norah paused, frowning. "From what I heard, Sissy Flagler paid a visit to Nate's photography studio and requested a sitting for photos of herself."

Ruthann swallowed. To say that Sissy had been aggressively hunting for a husband would be a kind way of putting it. Still, she couldn't imagine Nate finding an interest in Sissy Flagler. She was far too consumed with the trappings of wealth, and Nate . . . well, Nate simply seemed too humble for the likes of Sissy.

"She's saying that Nate sent her chaperone away—some woman her father apparently pays to accompany her about town. And that Nate took advantage of that opportunity, and . . . compromised her." The distaste with which Norah spoke the words was evident.

"No." It was all Ruthann could think to say. "He would never do such a thing."

"The word is that Sissy's father is now insisting they marry," Norah said quietly.

It felt as if Ruthann had swallowed an apple whole. She looked at Norah, horrified. "Surely Sissy isn't interested . . ." But she didn't finish the question. This was all far too convenient given Sissy's campaign for a husband over the past year. But why Nate?

Norah's hand wrapped around Ruthann's. "You still care for him."

Ruthann couldn't deny it. Norah knew her far too well. It didn't matter how many years had passed, or how many *would* pass, Nate Harper would have her heart. She nodded slowly.

"He doesn't have to agree to the arrangement," Norah said.

"He *does*. Can you imagine what Mr. Flagler will do to his business—to Nate's reputation—if he doesn't agree?" A sharp sadness rent itself though Ruthann. It wasn't fair to Nate at all. He'd come back here to his home to start his life anew.

And now he faced an unwilling marriage to the most odious woman imaginable.

"Why Nate?" she said aloud as the words ran through her mind again.

Norah shook her head. "Perhaps because he's only recently returned to town? That was Mrs. Bonner's thought. He hasn't been here long enough to know to avoid Sissy. Besides, he's young, and she's likely heard that he's a good man."

What would he do? Ruthann had no doubt that Mr. Flagler would see to it that Nate was run out of town if he refused Sissy's hand. And when she thought of that sadness that lurked behind Nate's eyes, it nearly tore her heart in two to imagine how Sissy's actions would hurt him even more.

"It isn't fair," she whispered.

"It isn't," Norah said. "But you're right. I don't know how he can fight it and manage to keep his reputation intact."

"Stuart," Ruthann said, pushing aside the desperation over Nate's situation in favor of hope. "He might know what to do. I must talk to him."

Norah nodded and quickly embraced Ruthann. "I hope he'll have a solution."

Ruthann could hardly keep herself from running the short distance to her family's home. She arrived, out of breath and clasping her hat to keep it from dipping sideways on her head, and flew through the rear door.

Voices echoed from down the hallway, the words incomprehensible but the men themselves unmistakable. Ruthann glanced at her mother, who was in the kitchen, rolling out dough for bread.

"Leave them be," Mama said, but Ruthann was already halfway down the hall, following the sound of Stuart's and Nate's voices.

She paused just outside the parlor door, ripping the hat from her head and pressing her hand against the wall as she listened and caught her breath.

Nate spoke, his voice laced with resignation. "I don't see another solution. I either marry this woman or leave town."

Ruthann sunk against the wall, closing her eyes.

It was over. Not that she had any claim on Nate, but if he was determined to marry Sissy, she would need to shutter that part of her heart that yearned for him. Forever. Somehow.

"There is one possibility," Stuart said.

Ruthann's eyes flew open. She *knew* Stuart would have an idea.

"But you won't like it."

Chapter Six

NATE SIGHED AND RAN a hand through his hair. Trust Stuart to have some farfetched idea that would get him out of marrying this Sissy Flagler or closing up his business altogether and leaving Cañon City.

His home.

He swallowed, trying to force down the despair that came with the idea of leaving again. Not much had felt right to him for the past several years, except photography and coming back to Cañon City. The moment he'd stepped off the train at the depot and breathed in the air here, he *knew* he'd made the right decision. Despite having no family of which to speak, his friends were here. And they'd welcomed him back with open arms.

"All right, what is it?" he asked Stuart.

Stuart gave him that half-grin he'd always sported when presenting some poorly conceived idea, whether it be climbing to the roof of the livery stable at midnight or riding bareback and nearly breaking their necks at thirteen. And now, apparently, his newest scheme would save Nate's future.

Maybe.

"It's simple, really," he said. "You lie."

"And say what?" Nate asked.

"You're already engaged to be married. And, as such, you can't possibly marry Miss Flagler." Nate leaned an arm against the fireplace mantel, clearly proud of his idea.

And it wasn't a bad one at all—*if* Nate had a woman to produce to prove it. "What happens when this pretend lady never appears and the marriage never happens?"

"You say she called it off. She won't be coming from the Dakota Territory—or wherever—after all."

Nate had a sneaking suspicion that Miss Flagler and her father wouldn't be so easily satisfied. "What if Mr. Flagler insists I end this so-called engagement immediately to marry his daughter?" It was exactly what would happen, judging from what Stuart had said about Miss Flagler's father. The man had money—a *lot* of money—and wasn't shy about using his standing in town to get what he wanted.

And if he wanted Nate ruined, it would happen.

Stuart apparently had the same thought, because he shook his head. "No, we need something better. Something Flagler can't oppose."

Nate crossed to the hearth to stand opposite Stuart. A fire burned low to ward off the chill that would come as the sun descended. He leaned his hands against the mantel and tried to think. But nothing would come.

"You can't marry Sissy Flagler," Stuart said for the second time that afternoon. "She'll make you miserable."

Nate pressed a hand to his forehead, closing his eyes against the dull thud of a growing headache. He'd felt no attraction whatsoever to Miss Flagler. In fact, he'd spent most of their photography session trying to keep her at arm's length. It had been night and day from when he'd taken Ruthann's photo. The time had passed far too quickly then.

No. No matter what happened with Miss Flagler, he had to keep Ruthann from his thoughts. Stuart would throttle him if he knew Nate thought of her in any way other than as a little sister.

He squeezed his fingers against his head, pushing the headache and the lingering image of Ruthann from his mind. "Perhaps if I told Mr. Flagler that I have nothing to my name, other than the studio?" He turned to face Stuart again. "Surely he wants his daughter to marry into wealth?"

Stuart shook his head. He shared the same eyes and the same hair color with Ruthann. *No.* Why was Nate thinking of Ruthann again?

"But if I told him I rented a room, had no home? No extra money to buy any comforts?" Nate felt as if he were grasping at the last shred of hope that existed.

"Flagler won't care, not now. Sissy's scared off every man her father would have chosen for her. He wants her married and out of trouble."

"Trouble?"

"There was a whiff of scandal a few months ago with a salesman who'd just arrived in town. But when Flagler got wind of it and tried to get that man to marry his daughter, he'd already gone. Can't blame the fellow, really," Stuart said.

"There's no way out of this." Nate stared into the fire and tried to imagine what his life was about to become.

"You could—"

"I'm *not* leaving town." Even if it meant being tied to the likes of Sissy Flagler, Nate was home. Cañon City was just as much his home as it was Flagler's, and he refused to leave.

Stuart sighed. "Then I don't—"

"I have an idea," a soft but strong voice said from somewhere behind Nate.

He whipped around to see Ruthann standing in the doorway. With wisps of hair falling gently around her face and her blue eyes wide and unassuming, she looked like an angel. His heart immediately tripped over itself, and his mind went right back to that moment six years ago when he'd summoned all the courage he possessed and kissed her.

Try as he might, kissing Ruthann Joliet was impossible to forget.

"Ruthann?" Stuart frowned at her. "I thought you were out?"

"Clearly I've returned," she said, a note of irritation in her voice. "And I know all about Nate's predicament."

Stuart slid Nate a look. "The gossipmongers are already at work, it seems."

Nate could picture the ladies in town whispering behind their hands and in their parlors—about *him*. He winced at the thought.

"It doesn't matter how I discovered it." Ruthann waved a hand. "But we must put a stop to it."

"We?" Stuart said, but Ruthann pointedly ignored him.

"Sissy Flagler is not a . . . kind woman," Ruthann said, clearly choosing her words very carefully. "Stuart was right when he said you needed a solution that her father couldn't tear apart. And I have an idea."

"By all means, let's hear it." Stuart's words held a note of brotherly irritation.

Ruthann shot a glare at him before folding her hands together and glancing at Nate and then down at the floor. She seemed suddenly shy, her pretty features tingeing pink. Nate pushed away the irrational urge to take her up into his arms.

She took a deep breath before looking up at them again. "Stuart had a good idea when he suggested you claim to be engaged, but that doesn't go far enough. What if you were already married?"

Nate furrowed his brow. "But I'm not."

Ruthann looked at him for a moment, and her meaning sunk in slowly.

"You mean him to make up a wife?" Stuart said, casting an incredulous glance at his sister. "That's an even bigger falsehood than I'd proposed."

"Yes, it is. But no. Maybe a little." She paused and drew in a breath. "He wouldn't be lying about having a wife—if he married immediately. Then he couldn't possibly marry Sissy. And his wife can say she was present in a back room while Sissy was at the studio. That part would be a lie, of course, but it's a good one, isn't it? To save Nate's business? It would be her word against Sissy's, and few people in this town will give credence to Sissy's story when another, more reputable woman says otherwise." Ruthann smiled, seemingly more brave now that she'd gotten the words out.

Stuart blinked and said nothing for a moment, while Nate could hardly catch the thoughts tumbling through his head.

Marry now.

But how?

And to whom?

A rising note of panic clawed its way up into his chest, choking off the ability to ask any of those questions out loud.

"How? And who would be the bride?" Stuart asked the questions for him.

"Surely any minister in this town wouldn't turn down a plea from a couple desperate to marry," Ruthann said.

Stuart nodded slowly. "And the lucky lady? Do you have someone in mind, Ruthie?"

The color in Ruthann's face deepened to scarlet, and Nate was certain his own face likely matched. Here they were, his oldest friend and the girl he'd kissed years ago, discussing a marriage of convenience to save his hide.

Who would want to marry *him*? A man so scarred by his past that it kept him awake at night?

"Well . . . perhaps," she said slowly. "Do keep in mind that the marriage can be annulled after Mr. Flagler's furor has ceased. After Sissy has moved along to place her claws in some other poor man."

Nate swallowed, a bit of his fear subsiding. An annulment. It wasn't something he'd ever planned. Then again, he wasn't certain he'd ever marry. No lady in her right mind would choose a man so haunted by his time fighting near the Black Hills. He couldn't expect a woman to take that on—to stand beside him as he wrestled with the nightmares and the memories. It wouldn't be fair.

"And?" Stuart pressed.

Ruthann clasped her hands together again, and Nate thought he saw her straighten as she lifted her chin.

"Me. I'd be willing," she said.

Chapter Seven

"NO," NATE AND STUART said at the exact same time.

Ruthann squeezed her hands together. She was prepared for a fight. But she wasn't ready for the look of terror on Nate's face.

Was the thought of marrying her so distasteful to him?

Well, there was no going back now, no matter how hard her heart beat and how much her fingers shook. She'd put the idea out there, and now she had to convince them.

"It's a good plan," she said. "You both know that. It's the only possibility, if Nate wishes to stay here and avoid an entanglement with Sissy."

"I don't deny that." Stuart's face had gone a furious red. "But under no circumstances did I expect you to offer yourself. I forbid it."

His words got under her skin and riled every part of her that valued her independence. "That isn't your decision to make, Stuart. I'm a grown woman. I know precisely what I'd be agreeing to."

Nate's face seemed to twist in fear at her words, and she bit her lip. Disappointment at his reaction crept through her. He'd certainly seemed comfortable with her the other day. So much so that she'd hoped . . . Well, she'd at least hoped he wouldn't be so horrified at her suggestion.

Stuart threw up his hands. "What about your prospects?"

"I have no prospects at the moment, brother," she said.

"Oh, that's right. Because not a one of them measured up to your lofty ideals, but here you are, willing to throw away any chance you have remaining." Stuart shoved his hands into his trouser pockets and paced across the room.

Ruthann moved her hands to her hips, any nerves forgotten now that she was sparring with her brother. "I have the opportunity to help a dear friend. Why wouldn't I offer?"

Stuart tossed a hand out, gesturing at Nate. "What if Nate declines? What if he doesn't wish to see you tied up in such a situation?"

They both turned to look at Nate, who'd gone as white as the snow in January.

"I can't," he finally said, his voice sounding as if it had been drug over rocks.

"See? He can't. It's a good idea, but find someone else, Ruthie," Stuart said.

Ruthann forced herself to look Nate in the eye, even as her heart plummeted and all she truly wished to do was rush away and forget she'd said anything. *Am I really so odious you can't fathom marrying me?* The question played out unspoken in her mind.

Nate held her gaze, and she knew then—she *knew*.

It wasn't because he found the thought of marrying her distasteful.

He was afraid.

Of what, she didn't know. Of her? Or marriage in general? Or of whatever it was that sat like a ghost behind his eyes?

"It would be only for as long it takes Sissy to entangle herself with someone else," she said softly. Out of the corner of her eye, Stuart shook his head, but Ruthann kept her attention on Nate. "It's the only way. You came home to be among friends. Let us help you."

He let out a shuddering breath and pressed the fingers of one hand to his forehead. "I don't know . . ."

"Are you seriously considering this—this—preposterous suggestion?" Stuart stared at Nate.

Nate cast a desperate glance at Stuart, who shook his head again. He *was* considering it. Ruthann drew in a breath. Might it actually happen?

Would she find herself married to Nate Harper, after all these years of dreaming about that one moment they shared?

"I don't know what else to do," Nate said to Stuart. "It would be a marriage in name only, that I can promise."

Ruthann didn't much like the sound of *that*, but once they spent more time together . . . once he kissed her again, maybe she could change his mind.

"I don't like it," Stuart said, but his stance was softening.

"I won't let any harm come to Ruthann. She's like a . . . a sister to me," Nate said.

Ruthann tried to take heart in the fact that Nate paused before saying "sister," as if he had to convince himself to think that way.

Stuart held his gaze, but said nothing.

"I can't leave," Nate said quietly.

And with those words, Stuart's expression changed. He closed his eyes, as if he was accepting the inevitable, and when he opened them, he gave a short nod.

"I thoroughly disapprove. But if it's the only possibility . . . then fine. Provided Ruthann is still agreeable?" Stuart looked at her.

"I am." She could feel Nate's eyes on her, that deep brown that could go warm or cold in an instant. She didn't dare look at him in case they were anything less than warm at the moment.

"And, I swear, Harper, if you lay a finger on her, I'll run you out of town myself." Stuart's tone left no room for argument.

"You have my word," Nate said to Ruthann's everlasting dismay.

She'd make Stuart see how happy she and Nate could make each other—if she could convince Nate first.

"Then I suppose we ought to get to the preacher," Stuart said in a resigned voice. "Do you want to tell Mama and Papa now, or later?"

"Later," Ruthann said immediately. As much as her parents wished for her to marry, and as much as they liked Nate, they wouldn't understand the haste of the wedding—unless they'd heard the gossip. And if that was the case, they would almost certainly refuse to let her go through with it.

When she was married, she could sit down with them and explain. And as much as they might protest, there would be no undoing it without an annulment . . . Ruthann cringed at the thought of them knowing Nate planned to annul the marriage as soon as possible.

Perhaps she would leave that part out. Especially considering she hoped to change his mind.

"Then let's get to a church before Mama catches wind of this insanity," Stuart said as he gestured to the door.

Ruthann glanced up at Nate as he held the door for her, but he looked straight ahead, every muscle in his face rigid.

She pressed her shoulders back, and then, just as she passed, he looked down. That fear was still there, but his eyes were like melted chocolate, and for just a moment, she thought she saw hope reflected in them.

He looked back up immediately, but Ruthann smiled to herself as she stepped outside.

He did care for her, as much as he wished to hide it. And by the time this day was over, she would be Mrs. Nathaniel Harper.

Then she could get to work showing him how much she adored him.

Chapter Eight

STUART AND NORAH PARKER were the only witnesses to the hasty wedding. They were halfway to the church when Stuart realized they needed a second witness, and Ruthann suggested Norah. They backtracked to the Parkers' home, which Nate remembered vividly from paying many visits with Jeremy and Stuart.

Norah in tow, they arrived at the nearest church. It wasn't the one that the Joliets normally attended, and Nate suspected Stuart had done that on purpose. They were in luck—the preacher was not only present, but more than willing to marry a "couple so in love," as he'd put it.

Nate had cringed some at the man's words, but Ruthann had smiled brightly at him. He'd then spent a solid ten minutes wondering if that smile was only to please the minister, or for some other reason Nate didn't dare entertain.

He hated doing this. Ruthann deserved so much better than a man like him. And yet at the same time, a part of him wanted to yelp in glee. That must be the nineteen-year-old version of himself, the boy who hadn't yet seen the horrors of the world. Whose most pressing worries were of when he might see his friend's little sister again and whether his mother had saved enough beef for that stew he liked.

Before he'd given in to the urge to kiss Ruthann. Before his mother had suddenly died. And before he'd made the worst decision of his life.

Now Ruthann looked up at him with all the innocent hope in the world as he held her small hands in his own and the minister spoke the words of the marriage ceremony. Stuart stood stiffly nearby, while Norah gazed at them in utter happiness. Nate wondered if she'd look so happy once her friend explained the truth of the situation to her.

Although with the way Ruthann was looking at him now, he could almost forget this was temporary. And he could almost forget what he'd promised Stuart.

Having Ruthann nearby all the time was going to try every shred of self-control Nate had, and the Army had ensured he had plenty of that.

He tried to keep a neutral expression, even as the minister pronounced them husband and wife. And it worked—until he was told he could kiss the bride.

Nate's mind spun. How could he have forgotten this would be part of the ceremony? Stuart shot daggers at him with his eyes while Norah clasped her hands to her chest.

And Ruthann . . . His new bride bit her lip before giving him an encouraging smile. He wondered if she was thinking of that moment by the river, six years ago.

The seconds stretched out, and Nate didn't think he could take one more moment of everyone staring at them expectantly. Best to get it done with.

He leaned down and pressed a short, chaste kiss to Ruthann's lips. She sighed, ever so slightly, and he had to force himself to lift his head instead of wrapping his arms around her and kissing her thoroughly, the way he'd dreamed of almost daily for years.

"Congratulations," the minister said, reaching out his hand.

Nate took it and thanked the man as Norah joined Ruthann. They whispered among themselves, and he strained to hear the words.

As the minister went to speak with Ruthann, Stuart stepped between Nate and the ladies. "Now onto a more pressing matter. Where precisely do you intend to live with my sister?"

Where did he intend to live? Nate grimaced. Surely he couldn't bring Ruthann back to his room at the boardinghouse. Not only wasn't it fit for ladies, it was only one room.

"There is an apartment built over top of my studio," he said, trying to remember what it looked like the one time he went up there. He quickly fetched a few items for the studio and then ran from the mess upstairs. It was probably best not to convey how dirty it truly was to Stuart. "It's furnished. It isn't much, but it's more amenable than the boardinghouse."

Stuart nodded as Ruthann and Norah joined them.

"Nate has decided that the rooms over his studio will be suitable lodgings," Stuart said to Ruthann.

Nate wasn't certain how he expected Ruthann to react, but she nodded. Of course she wouldn't complain. She was far too level-headed, and besides, this was only a temporary arrangement. And as Ruthann looked up at him with her generous smile, he knew he'd need to remind himself of that fact again and again.

"Norah will help me pack my things. I suppose you'll need to return with us too, in order to convey the news to my parents? Then we can return to your studio." Her voice was even, and—although Nate was sure he was imagining it—almost eager. As if she couldn't wait to join him.

He dug his fingertips into his palms. Thinking like that would get him nowhere but disappointed. Or in a heap of trouble.

He agreed to her suggestion although he did not at all look forward to informing Mr. and Mrs. Joliet that he'd married their daughter without their knowledge or consent. They'd been almost like second parents to him, and he cringed as he imagined their reaction to the news.

As they left the church and turned toward Ruthann and Stuart's home, Nate drew in the fresh, outdoor air to clear his head. Ruthann was as beautiful as ever, and kinder than he deserved. She was willing to do him the greatest favor ever granted him—as a *friend*. He repeated that word, the one she'd used back in the parlor at her parents' home, over and over as they walked.

To read anything more into her actions or those looks she gave him was folly. Besides, even if she did harbor some feelings for him that were more than friendship, he'd do her no good with returning them. No woman, particularly not one as charitable as Ruthann, deserved a man like Nate. He'd seen too much, and it would never, *never* leave him.

Upon arriving at the Joliets' home, he didn't have any more time to worry on how Ruthann's parents might react. Because they were both waiting in the parlor.

They *knew* something was afoot, that much was clear from the rigidity of how they sat and the suspicious look Mr. Joliet gave the lot of them. The man stood immediately.

"Miss Parker," he said, nodding at Norah. "Nate Harper. It's good to see you back in town." He extended a hand, and Nate shook it as rivers of guilt traveled through him from head to toe. The Joliets had always been so kind to him, letting him stay for dinner and sneaking extra bits of venison and biscuits into a basket that they insisted he bring home to his mother.

And now he was repaying them for those years of generosity by running off to marry their daughter.

"I am happy to see you again, Nate," Mrs. Joliet said with a warm smile. "But I would like to know what's behind all of these whispers and sneaking off."

Mr. Joliet raised his eyebrows as he looked at each of them in turn.

"Nate was in a—" Stuart began, but Nate stepped forward and cut him off.

"Miss Joliet—Ruthann—and I have married." There was nothing to do but to be as honest as possible. He extended a hand to Ruthann, who gave him a tentative smile even as her eyes flicked toward her father.

Mr. Joliet stared at them while his wife clasped her hands together.

"You knew about this?" Mr. Joliet asked Stuart.

"Yes, sir." Stuart shifted uncomfortably. "I—well, I—"

"We couldn't wait another moment," Ruthann said, gazing up at Nate with an expression of pure joy. Was it real? Or was it only for show? He'd be a fool to assume her true feelings were reflected in that radiant look she gave him.

"I'm afraid Stuart and I were so delighted with the news that we suggested they not delay a wedding," Norah added. She was clearly trying to pull some of the blame for the hasty marriage off of Ruthann and Nate, and Ruthann gave her a grateful look even as Stuart frowned.

"Oh, Mama." Ruthann dropped Nate's hand and took up her mother's, who looked on the verge of tears. "I'm sorry. I know you would have wanted to be involved. But that would have meant a long engagement, and we, well . . . we . . ." Her eyes found Nate's, begging for help.

He cleared his throat. "We couldn't stand to be apart any longer." Being untruthful to the Joliets wasn't easy, and yet, he'd thought of Ruthann every day of those years he'd been away. His words held more truth than he'd ever admit.

"Yes," Ruthann said warmly, her blue eyes on him, holding him in place and making it difficult for him to breathe.

How was he ever going to survive days, weeks, or even months of that look without taking her hands and pulling her to him? He swallowed hard and glanced down at his feet until the feeling passed.

"Well," Mrs. Joliet said, her voice trembling just a little. "I suppose congratulations are in order. Aren't they, Terrence? We've waited for this day for quite some time." She looked to her husband.

Mr. Joliet said nothing for a moment, fixing a stern gaze onto Nate. It would be easy to crumple under the man's stare, but Nate had survived worse in his years in the Army. Not to mention the looks Stuart had already given him today. Even a glare straight from Lucifer himself couldn't match the one that Stuart seemed to have permanently fixed on his face. Nate straightened his back and held Mr. Joliet's gaze. Finally, the man nodded and his angry, protective expression eased into something bordering on resigned acceptance.

He might not have been happy about how the union had happened, but at least he seemed less enraged.

Nate spent an awkward hour with Stuart and the Joliets while Norah helped Ruthann gather up her necessities. He quickly promised to hire a wagon to retrieve anything else tomorrow, and he invited the Joliets to sit for their photograph for no charge. While Mrs. Joliet was delighted with all of it, the dour expression never left her husband's face.

"I believe he despises me now," Nate said to Stuart when Mrs. Joliet went upstairs to see how the girls were getting along and Mr. Joliet excused himself to a prior engagement Nate doubted truly existed.

"He'll come around," Stuart said. "It's the haste—and the fact that you didn't speak to him first—that bothers him. My mother will persuade him."

Nate hoped Mrs. Joliet might smooth things over. The last thing he wanted was to lose the affection of a man who'd always been like an uncle to him, particularly when he didn't have any family of his own to count on.

Although, he mused, the Joliets *were* his family now. The thought settled like a warm blanket around his mind.

It's temporary, he reminded himself. Best not to become too comfortable with the idea. Especially when—

Nate cringed at the thought that had run through his mind. "They'll want nothing at all to do with me when this is over."

Stuart pressed his lips together and then frowned. "I don't know how they'll take it." It was an optimistic statement, meant to make him feel better.

But instead, he felt as if he'd swallowed dust.

"Come, let's fetch a carriage. Ruthann is certain to bring half her belongings," Stuart said.

Nate nodded, glad for the distraction from his thoughts.

When they returned, the ladies were descending the stairs. The two younger women each carried a heavy-looking carpetbag, which Nate and Stuart collected from them.

"What are you bringing for one night, the entire contents of the silver drawer?" Stuart grumbled as he hefted the carpetbag onto his shoulder.

Ruthann gave him a withering look before turning to Nate, who received a bright smile instead. "I believe we're ready to go." She laid a hand gently on Nate's arm, and Mrs. Joliet beamed.

It was only for show. Nate gritted his teeth as he reminded himself of that. All too soon, the soft pressure from Ruthann's hand was gone, and they were outside. He assisted her into the carriage, intentionally avoiding looking into her eyes as she took his hand.

Stuart loaded the two bags, Norah and Mrs. Joliet offered Ruthann hugs and kisses on the cheek, and then they were off.

Headed toward home. Together. Because somehow, Ruthann Joliet was now Ruthann Harper.

His wife.

It was as if God had reached into the recesses of his mind, plucked out the one wish Nate knew he could never have, and given it to him.

And as he glanced at Ruthann, who met his gaze with the sweetest, most wonderful smile he'd ever seen, Nate knew he faced the impossible.

How could he avoid falling in love with someone he'd never stopped loving?

Chapter Nine

"OH."

It was the only word that came to Ruthann's mind when Nate led her up the stairs and threw open the door to the little apartment.

The room they walked into, a small parlor, looked as if it had never seen a broom, much less a speck of water.

"It's . . . well." Nate rubbed his hand across his chin, a habit Ruthann remembered well from their childhood. It was just as endearing now as it had been then.

"It just needs a little cleaning," Ruthann said. The last thing she wanted was Nate feeling badly about this place. She ran a hand over the dusty back of a wing chair. "The furniture is good. And look at the size of that fireplace. We'll never go cold in winter."

She turned away and squeezed her eyes shut the second the words were out of her mouth. It was June, and here she was thinking—and saying out loud—that they'd still be married come winter.

But Nate said nothing about that, instead moving to a door to the right. "I believe this is the kitchen."

Ruthann peered around him, into a dirty and sparsely furnished, but functional-looking kitchen. And then, in front of the building, on the far side of the parlor was a bedroom.

The *only* bedroom.

A flush crept up Ruthann's cheeks as she surveyed the bed that needed airing out, a single chair, and a small stand of drawers with a washbasin and pitcher she didn't dare look into.

They'd agreed this was a marriage in name only. And as much as Ruthann wished to be married to Nate for love, she wasn't certain she was ready for anything more than another kiss.

"I'll sleep in the parlor," he said quickly, as if he were reading her thoughts.

Ruthann nodded, although she wondered how his long frame would fit comfortably on that settee. "We'll need some supplies. Food, of course, and dishes, pots, and pans. A broom, a scrubbing brush, some rags, clean linens . . ." She listed off a few more necessities.

Nate nodded. "Make a list, and I'll take it to the general store when I go out to collect my things from the boardinghouse. There is a broom downstairs, and a few rags, but not much else, I'm afraid."

"I'll ask Mrs. Claver next door if I can't borrow a few things," Ruthann said, glancing around the parlor again, this time with a more critical eye. Mrs. Claver wouldn't hesitate to help her out. "She used to give me penny candy each time Mama took me in for a new hat."

"My mother spoke highly of her," Nate said.

When Ruthann glanced up at him, he seemed lost in thought. "You must miss her so much," she said gently.

He swallowed, his Adam's apple bobbing as he pressed his hands to his hips. "I do."

"She was a remarkable woman." Ruthann hadn't often seen her on social calls because Mrs. Harper had worked long hours to keep her only son fed and clothed and with a roof over his head. But she had raised him well, all on her own, and was always as gracious and giving as she could be.

Nate gave her a tight smile, and Ruthann hoped she hadn't caused him too much sadness by speaking of her.

"I'll speak with Mrs. Claver now," she said, gathering her skirts and moving toward the door that led to the stairs. Her carpetbags sat just inside the door; but she hated to unpack without giving the place as much of a scrubbing as she could before it grew too late in the day.

"I apologize for the state of the place," Nate said as they returned downstairs. "I doubt any woman wishes to undertake a thorough cleaning of an apartment on her wedding day."

Ruthann laughed. "Well, I suppose that with such an untraditional marriage, we ought to start things off as unexpectedly as possible."

That drew a grin from him, and her heart danced at his lightened mood. He gathered his hat and stood by the door, turning it over in his hands. "I suppose I ought to pay Mr. Flagler a visit."

"There is no need, unless you desire to be the one to give him the news. My mother and Norah will ensure the entire town knows you're married before sunset." And then, thankfully, this nightmare would end for Nate.

After Ruthann paid her own visit to Sissy, anyway.

Nate made his way to the general store while Ruthann turned toward Mrs. Claver's hat shop next door. Visiting Sissy Flagler—and lying about having overheard the photography session she'd had with Nate—was not something Ruthann looked forward to at all, and yet it was the only way she could ensure the woman knew that any hold she thought she had over Nate was gone.

Mrs. Claver was more than willing to help, and Ruthann left her shop armed with every cleaning item she could possibly need. She filled the bucket with water from the well behind the businesses, and after lugging everything upstairs, she set to work.

By the time Nate returned, she'd accomplished what was necessary for that evening. The rest would simply have to wait until tomorrow. As Nate brought in crates filled with food and other items, Ruthann delighted in the simple task of unpacking each thing.

How funny it was that she could tear open brown paper with such glee, knowing the surprise inside was something so practical. It wasn't as if she grew giddy at the thought of putting away flour and salt at her parents' home.

But this was all hers. Hers and Nate's, to share. She would decide where the tin of crackers would be kept, and where she'd hide the scrub brush, and how neatly the bed would be made.

She smiled at a basket of eggs before letting her eyes sweep over the room to figure out where to keep it.

"I believe this is the last item." Nate set a small parcel in the middle of the rickety table that Ruthann had scrubbed clean earlier.

Setting down the eggs, Ruthann took up the parcel and pulled the string. Inside sat a small, hinged wooden box. Curious, Ruthann lifted the tiny lid—to discover a cameo brooch resting on a velvet cushion.

Her hand pressed to her chest, Ruthann lifted her eyes to meet Nate's. "It's lovely. I— I don't know what to say."

The corners of his mouth lifted. "You don't have to say anything. I thought . . . Well, you deserved something nice."

It was a wedding gift, Ruthann realized as heat flooded her face. For her. She gazed down at the brooch again and ran a finger over the fine workmanship. Could Nate afford such a thing? She didn't dare ask, for fear of insulting him. Yet, she didn't want him to feel as if she required such fancy things.

She looked up to find him watching her. He was likely waiting to see her put it on. She picked it up and realized the problem she faced.

"I fear I can't pin it properly without a looking glass. And there isn't one to be found here."

"I have one downstairs for customers to use. I'll bring it up until we can purchase a second one," he said, stepping forward and taking the cameo from her hand. "May I?"

Ruthann nodded, and he reached out to pin the brooch to her dress. His fingers grazed her chin ever-so-softly, and she froze in place.

"There," he said. "Beautiful."

She wasn't certain if he was talking about the brooch or *her*. She pressed her hands into her skirts. "Thank you. I . . ." She cast about for something to say. Something to make him stop looking at her so intensely. It was almost more than she could take, that look. "I haven't finished cleaning, but I accomplished enough to make it livable for the night."

He drew his gaze from her to the rest of the kitchen, and suddenly Ruthann wished he'd look at her with those dark eyes again.

"It looks nice," he said. "Thank you."

"It wasn't anything." She didn't want him thinking she was afraid of hard work. "It will be no time at all until this is a comfortable home."

At that last word—*home*—Nate stiffened, drawing his shoulders back. "It won't be long before you can return to your own home. I promise I won't keep you in this situation longer than is necessary."

Ruthann pressed her lips together, hoping her face didn't betray her emotions.

"I have some work to finish downstairs," Nate said.

"All right." Ruthann had to force the words out. "I'll make supper."

And then he was gone. Her fingers drifted to the pretty new brooch. When she'd opened it, it had taken her by surprise. And when he'd pinned it to her dress, she'd thought it might have meant something.

But perhaps it was only an apology for him needing her as his wife.

Ruthann sighed, all the hope she'd gathered up in such a short time falling away—again. Had she imagined the way he'd looked at her?

She hadn't. She *knew* she hadn't. Then why did he close the door on those feelings so quickly?

She was more certain than ever that something had happened to him in the Dakota Territory. If only he'd trust her enough to tell her what it was.

Then maybe—just maybe—they might have a chance at a real marriage.

Chapter Ten

NATE WOKE WITH A CRICK in his neck and an ache in his back. The settee was the most uncomfortable place he'd ever laid his head, and considering how many nights he'd spent sleeping on a bedroll on the ground, that was saying something.

It was early yet, and all was quiet from behind the bedroom door. He hoped Ruthann had slept well. He couldn't say the same for himself. And it wasn't just because of the settee.

Every time he'd begun to drift off, his mind wandered to Ruthann. She was so close, and yet he'd purposely kept her far away.

He rubbed his neck as he cringed at the memory of the night before. He'd gone too far, buying her that brooch. But he couldn't resist when he'd seen it.

And then he'd pinned it to her dress.

Just the slightest feel of her warm skin against his fingers had sent his head spinning. He'd had to back off—or he feared what might come next.

He wouldn't do that to Ruthann—let her care for someone like him. It wouldn't be right.

But she'd seemed a bit distant last night at supper, and he feared he'd gone too cold toward her. That wouldn't do either, especially considering all she'd done for him. Not to mention how much it hurt him to keep her at such a distance.

Changing quickly, he made his way downstairs to look again at the photographs he'd developed yesterday. Several of them had turned out better than he'd expected, and, as usually happened, he became lost in the work until a soft voice interrupted him.

"Nate? I've breakfast ready, if you're hungry." Ruthann stood outside the open door to his darkroom, her fingers clutching the doorframe as if she were uncertain about whether to disturb him.

Nate set the photo in his hand down as his stomach grumbled silently. Ruthann's dark blonde hair was swept up in a style that sent a few wisps loose around her face. His fingers itched to press them back, to run the pad of his thumb over the worry line in her forehead. Instead, he clenched his hands against his sides and gave a short nod, knowing he was the one responsible for that worry line and the cautious way she stood outside the door.

"I am, thank you." He needed to apologize. Perhaps then he'd see the sweet, carefree side of Ruthann again.

But how? What could he say? *Ruthann, I'm sorry I was cold to you. I'm afraid I'll fall in love with you—again. And I don't want you to fall in love with me.*

That wouldn't do, clearly.

He had just begun to follow her up the stairs when the front door to the studio opened.

Miss Flagler and her chaperone stood in his doorway.

Nate stopped still. Miss Flagler was the last person he'd expected to see. He glanced at Ruthann, whose eyes widened as they went from Miss Flagler to him.

"Good morning, Miss Flagler." He tried to banish the hesitancy from his voice and nodded at the woman's chaperone, to whom he'd not been introduced. Although he didn't want to, he returned to the bottom of the stairs. He didn't have to see Ruthann to know she was right behind them, and he was grateful for her presence.

"Mr. Harper," the younger woman said, a note of irritation lacing her voice. She glanced behind him. "Ruthann."

Ruthann came around to his side, and when he glanced at her, she held her chin high, strength evident in every part of her stance. "It's good to see you again, Sissy," she said warmly.

"Yes, I hope you are well," Miss Flagler said in a voice that said otherwise.

But to Ruthann's credit, her serene smile didn't falter even a bit.

Miss Flagler glanced at her chaperone, who nodded impatiently.

"Congratulations on your wedding," Miss Flagler said as primly as possible. "I imagine Mr. Harper told you about our . . . photography session?"

She was looking to find out how much Ruthann knew—or was taunting her. Nate clenched his jaw.

But Ruthann smoothed her skirts, that placid smile never leaving her face. "He did. But he needn't have. Nate and I have spent most all of our time together lately." She glanced up at him, her eyes conveying a peacefulness he couldn't begin to fathom in this moment. And then she reached for his hand.

Sliding her fingers through his, she turned her attention back to Miss Flagler—whose mouth had opened ever so slightly in obvious surprise.

Ruthann didn't have to resort to telling a falsehood. All she'd needed to do was imply her presence, and Miss Flagler had pieced it together herself.

"I see." Miss Flagler was *not* happy with this news, that much was apparent by the way she held herself, rigid but just barely holding back her anger.

Nate reluctantly let Ruthann's hand go and moved back toward his darkroom. "I have your photographs." He collected the two best from the table and brought them to Miss Flagler.

She took them with barely a glance.

"I hope you'll accept them as a gift, from Ruthann and myself." He doubted she cared much at all about the photographs, but simply giving them to her was easier than demanding payment. Now perhaps she would leave quietly.

Miss Flagler narrowed her eyes a moment as she looked at him, almost as if she were searching for something. Then she gave him a forced smile. "Thank you. That is very kind."

"Please, Sissy, I hope you'll come for tea soon," Ruthann said.

Nate jerked his head toward her. What could she possibly be thinking, inviting this viper for a social call? But Ruthann's face conveyed nothing that would explain her invitation.

Miss Flagler paused a moment. "Why, yes. That would be nice. I'll see you soon." She glanced again at Nate before following her chaperone out the door.

Upstairs, Ruthann had laid out a hearty breakfast of eggs, sausage, and thick slices of bread with butter and jam. Nate gazed at it longingly.

"Please, eat before it gets colder." Ruthann poured two steaming cups of coffee and set them down by each plate.

As hungry as he was, Nate paused a moment to pull out her chair. She gave him a gracious smile.

Those smiles would undo him, if he let them.

He forced his mind back to the food. It was just as good as it looked—fluffy eggs with just the right amount of salt, savory sausage, and the bread with sweet jam to accompany it all.

Ruthann had barely made a dent in hers before Nate cleared his plate.

"There is more," she said, eying his empty plate.

She didn't need to tell him twice. He filled his plate again.

"Thank you," he finally remembered to say. "This is the best breakfast I've had in a long time."

Her cheeks went a pleasing pink color. "I'm glad. What do you normally eat for breakfast?"

"Coffee."

She laughed then. "That's not a breakfast."

He grinned. It was impossible not to feel as if some weight had been lifted from his shoulders when he was with Ruthann. She was like sunshine through a storm. Speaking of storms . . .

He set his fork down for a moment. "You invited Miss Flagler for tea?"

She swallowed a bite of eggs. "I thought it might smooth things over for her. She's struggled since her family came here. Honestly, I don't believe she has many friends."

That wasn't hard to imagine. "It feels a bit reckless, having her here." *In our home*, he wanted to say, but the words felt too intimate in his mind.

"It will be just fine. We'll speak of parties and the latest fashions, and so long as you don't go calling me *Miss Joliet,* it will all go well."

"Well, I wouldn't call you Miss Joliet when you're Mrs. Harper now." Nate didn't know what possessed him to say it, but the words made her face redden again.

Exactly how much joy could a man derive from making a lady blush? He couldn't seem to stop.

"Yes, that is true," she said, her eggs seemingly forgotten as she looked up at him.

Those incredible blue eyes had likely never seen true worry, never mind fear or sadness. It made him feel wildly protective of her, as if he'd fight anyone who ever tried to bring her a moment of distress.

Of course, he'd been the one doing exactly that last evening.

"Ruthann." He turned in his chair to face her. He wanted to reach out and take one of her hands, to cradle it in his, but he didn't dare. "I owe you an apology for last night. I was short with you, and withdrawn, and I hope you'll forgive me."

"Of course I will." She paused, twisting those hands he so badly wanted to hold in her lap. "May I ask what was on your mind?"

Nate clenched his jaw. What could he tell her? That he feared falling in love with her—again? That he didn't want her to care so much about him? That every night for years, he dreamed of horrors he'd never contemplate detailing to her? That what he'd seen five years ago in the Dakota Territory had shaken him to his very core and made him question who he really was? That he could never think of a way to repay her for the kindness she'd done him, other than to set her free as soon as possible so she could find a better man to marry?

"It's nothing you need worry about," he finally said.

She watched him a moment longer, her eyes tracing his face as if she might find the answer there. Then, ever so gently, she rested a hand on his arm.

Nate's entire body stilled, not wanting to miss a moment of the way her soft fingers felt through the fabric of his shirt sleeve.

"Please know you can share anything with me," she said. "I'm an excellent confidant. Goodness knows I've helped Norah through a trying time, and even Stuart would admit to sharing a few confidences with me over the years."

She gave him that sweet smile again, and all it would take was just a second of doubt before he spilled everything to her willing ears.

He *couldn't* do that. Not only would he be baring feelings he'd had for her for years, he refused to let her know of the things he'd seen. Those were memories best kept sealed tightly, deep inside, so they wouldn't disturb this new life he was creating.

So instead, he wrapped his own hand around hers, reveling for just a second in the touch of her skin, before removing it and standing.

"Thank you," he said awkwardly. "I'll be downstairs. Please let me know if you find yourself in need of anything."

And with that, he closed the door to the apartment, and the strong urge to confess all his deepest thoughts to Ruthann.

Chapter Eleven

THE DAYS PASSED IN a blur of cleaning, cooking, and shopping. Ruthann feared spending too much at the general store, but Nate seemed not to mind her endless requests for much-needed household items.

It was hard to remember that this was only temporary when she caught him gazing at her with something akin to longing in his eyes. And then, just before she could wonder at it, he would smile at her. Perhaps he was as happy as she was with this arrangement. Which meant there was a chance this could turn into something real.

Sunday morning dawned bright and cheerful, and Ruthann found herself almost skipping down the stairs to Nate's studio. He waited for her near the door, hat in his hand. She might have imagined it, but Ruthann thought she saw his eyes widen just slightly.

But he immediately tugged on the edges of his jacket and said, "You look very nice," in a perfectly even tone.

"Thank you." His words warmed her, and she stepped forward with confidence.

Nate opened the door. Ruthann welcomed the sunshine. The morning chill had almost burned off for the day. She would likely need to shed her shawl before they arrived at the church.

The church. It would be the first time they'd be seen together in public. A shiver ran through Ruthann at the thought of all those eyes on them.

"Are you cold?" Nate asked as he shut the door to the studio.

"Oh, no." Ruthann adjusted her shawl.

He held out an arm, and she wrapped her own arm around his. She couldn't help but smile, but she looked away, embarrassed for him to see how happy such a simple gesture made her.

A few friends had stopped by to visit during the week to congratulate her on the marriage, but so many more people would see them together today. And considering their unconventional wedding, they were certain to attract attention.

Ruthann glanced up at Nate as they walked. He was so very careful—almost withdrawn at times. She was growing more used to this new Nate, and she feared the notice they'd most certainly draw at church might be too much for him.

"Nate?"

He looked down at her. It took her half a moment to remember what she wanted to say with the way he gazed at her.

"I have a feeling we'll be more interesting than Pastor Findley's sermon today. To the others at church, I mean," she said.

He drew in a deep breath as they rounded a corner. "I believe you're correct. If you'd like to leave at any time, all you have to do is say so."

It took Ruthann a moment to comprehend that he was worried about *her*. She pressed her free hand to her lips to contain a wild giggle that tried to escape. What she really wanted to do was throw her arms around him and bury her face in his neck, right here on the street on a Sunday morning.

Get a hold of yourself, a voice in her head demanded.

Ruthann dropped her hand and turned to Nate again. He was looking straight ahead now, his shoulders held back stiffly. She squeezed his arm with her hand. "Thank you. And I'm willing to leave early too, if you decide you'd like to."

He looked down at her again, almost in surprise. Then his face softened, and he nodded once, quickly.

When they arrived at the church, Mama, Papa, and Stuart were waiting outside. Ruthann was so grateful to see them, she could have melted out here among the trampled spring grasses and little wildflowers. Walking into church with her family would afford Nate some protection from the curious stares.

And stare they did.

Most were friendly, and those who weren't—Ruthann suspected—were more concerned about why she'd chosen to marry a man who'd been gone for more years than they remembered. She met each one with a gracious smile and a nod of her head.

Nate, she noticed, looked mostly straight ahead. But he seemed in control, and far less worried than she thought he'd seemed as they'd walked here.

She slid into a pew after Mama. It was their regular pew, right behind Norah's family.

Norah turned as they sat. "Ruthann, Nate! It's good to see you." She lowered her voice. "And you've survived everyone's curiosity."

Ruthann smiled, grateful for her friend's acknowledgment of the awkward situation. Even Nate seemed to relax now that it was spoken aloud. Stuart whispered something to him that brought a smile to his face, and Ruthann was filled with gratitude for both her brother and Norah. How could they ever feel uneasy with those they loved surrounding them?

They stood as the service began with singing. Nate sung along silently, but Ruthann let her voice mingle with everyone around them. Throughout the service, Ruthann's mind bounced between soaking in the words and being conscious of every slight movement Nate made.

They sat so close together in the pew that Ruthann thought she could feel the warmth from his body, and she yearned for him to reach over and take her hand. The thought wouldn't go away, even as she silently scolded herself for thinking such things during a church service, when her mind should be focused only on the service itself.

As the congregation stood to sing again, her wish was granted when Nate grasped hold of her hand. Ruthann nearly gasped out loud. She hardly dared venture a look at Nate, but curiosity got the better of her, and halfway through the joyous hymn, she turned her head ever so slightly to see him.

He was looking right at her.

Ruthann tripped over the words to the song as she quickly looked down. Hopefully he didn't notice how surprised she was, but a furious heat overtook her cheeks even as she tried to continue singing.

Was it possible Nate still harbored feelings for her?

The idea was almost too overwhelming to consider here in the church, with everyone around them.

When the hymn finished, Nate ran a thumb over the back of her hand before letting go. Her skin seemed to tingle at the memory of his touch, and Ruthann thought she'd never forget the feeling, not as long as she lived.

The moment they left the pew, old friends, acquaintances, and people she hardly knew began to gather around to congratulate them and wish them well. Ruthann forced her mind back to the present, and with Norah and Mama flanking her on one side and Nate on the other, she greeted each person.

It truly was wonderful to know how much each one of them cared. And while she was certain most wondered why they'd married so quickly, not a soul mentioned the haste of the wedding.

Ruthann glanced at Nate often, taking note of how he stood and the look on his face as he spoke with everyone who stopped by. Stuart stood beside him, taking on a good part of the conversation, and seemingly putting Nate at a greater ease then he might have otherwise been. She wondered if he'd noticed Nate take her hand, and decided he must not have, or else he wouldn't be smiling so broadly.

As the last of the congregation filtered by, she spotted someone watching from a distance—Sissy Flagler. The moment Ruthann caught her eye, Sissy's frown turned into a smile. She didn't come to greet them, instead turning back toward her father as they left the church.

Ruthann imagined Sissy still harbored sore feelings that her plan didn't work out as she'd hoped. And there wasn't much Ruthann could do about that except be as friendly as possible toward Sissy. Besides, as Norah had reminded Ruthann when she'd come to visit yesterday, Sissy's attention would turn elsewhere as soon as she found a new man to pin her attentions onto.

They were some of the last people out of the church. Mama and Papa insisted Nate and Ruthann join them for Sunday dinner, to which Ruthann quickly agreed, considering she hadn't thought to start anything before leaving for church. They whiled away a comfortable couple of hours, enjoying Mama's cooking and the company of family. Watching Nate and Stuart in the parlor after the meal, Ruthann thought she hadn't seen Nate more content since his arrival back in town.

When they left her parents' home, Nate paused just outside the door and turned to Ruthann. "What would you say to a stroll along the river?"

"That sounds lovely." Her heart leapt at the thought of spending time with him—and at his request. Besides, she wasn't particularly looking forward to the housework that awaited her back at their apartment. She'd scoured the rooms from top to bottom all week, and now the regular work of laundering and dusting and sweeping needed doing.

They walked side-by-side past homes and businesses that were closed for the day. A light breeze ruffled wisps of Ruthann's hair, and they nodded to other townsfolk who meandered along on their own Sunday strolls. They followed Eighth Street toward the river, passing the depot and climbing over the railroad tracks. Turning west to avoid the Smelting Works, they walked slowly along the riverbank.

"It's awfully fast today," Ruthann said, looking down at the brown and blue water churning quickly just below them.

Nate had paused, his gaze on the river. "I missed this. The spring melt, fishing, wading, seeing it become icy. All of it."

His eyes held a faraway look, as if he were thinking of all the happy times he'd spent by this river. Ruthann smiled as one memory in particular surfaced in her own mind.

"I don't suppose you're nostalgic for pushing a friend's sister into the muck?"

He blinked at her and then a smile split his expression. Laughing, he raised his hands. "If I remember correctly, I didn't do the pushing. That was your brother."

"Yes, but you egged him on," Ruthann said primly. "And I got in such trouble for ruining my dress."

Nate tilted his head. "As I remember, you got your revenge soon after. My hair smelled like rotten eggs for a week."

Ruthann grinned at the memory. She couldn't remember where she'd *found* the rotten eggs, but the childish zeal at getting back at her brother and Nate was as clear a memory as if it had happened yesterday.

They walked along, the railroad tracks and the town off to their right, and the hurried river to the left. The scent of spring was all around, fresh and new and full of promise. When Ruthann looked up at Nate again, his eyes had closed briefly as he seemed to breathe it all in.

Ruthann paused next to him. He seemed at peace for the moment, as if the past six years had never happened. "I'm glad you returned home," she said, trying to push the hesitancy out of her voice. If she were honest with him, perhaps he would be the same with her.

He glanced down at her and smiled. "I am too."

Ruthann's heart skipped. The way he looked at her as he said those words . . . Was he happy to be home *because* of her?

Before she could determine what to say in return, his hand found hers, his fingers winding in between her own.

Ruthann drew in a breath. This was different from when he took her hand in church. There, it had been reassuring, combining them in a united front against the curious looks of everyone around them. But out here . . . It served no purpose other than to show affection.

Could he know how deliriously happy this simple gesture made her? It was as if nothing existed aside from their two hands, wound together.

"I don't know how or why," he said. "But being with you makes the memories I'd rather forget fade somewhat."

"The memories from the time you were away?" she asked gently. She didn't know what had happened that had changed him so much, but it was ever-present, always lurking in the shadows behind his carefully chosen words and guarded smiles.

He nodded. And then smiled, not in as carefree a way as he did at nineteen, but instead tinged with a sadness that Ruthann ached to understand. But it was a smile nonetheless, and with it, he raised a hand and pressed a stray lock of hair behind her ear. His fingertips grazed her cheekbone, and Ruthann shivered.

Nate smiled again, the ghost of the past less evident this time, and they continued on their way. As the water churned and raced below, Ruthann found her thoughts strangely anchored. And her heart blossomed with hope.

Her marriage to Nate felt more real today than ever. Was it possible that the dream she'd held so close to her heart for so long could come true? Nate kept so much inside. Ruthann knew she'd barely scratched the surface. Did she dare imagine that one of those feelings he held so closely guarded might be love for her?

And just as the thought crossed her mind, a crack of thunder sounded in the distance.

Ruthann jumped—and so did Nate. Behind them, the sky had grown dark, and the gentle breeze turned into a wind.

And then the rain came, as fast as the river below them. Ruthann squealed in surprise as the drops began to fall. Looking up at Nate—who appeared just as surprised—she began to laugh.

Nate laughed too, with a reckless abandon that made Ruthann's heart soar, despite how soaked her clothing was becoming. He tugged her hand, and they began to run.

Back home, together.

Chapter Twelve

THE BEST PART OF NATE'S day came each evening, when he locked the door to the studio, ensured his equipment was safely stored for the night, and returned upstairs—to Ruthann.

Each evening, he paused outside the door at the top of the stairs, fighting the eager way he wished to open it and rush inside.

It isn't right.

She deserves better.

Whatever you do, don't promise too much.

The thoughts were logical and he ought to follow those directives. He *knew* that.

And yet, each evening, her sweet smile lit up when she saw him, and every part of the will he'd found outside the door slowly slid away.

Simply put, it was impossible to keep a hard heart when Ruthann was nearby. Particularly when she looked at him as if she held all the esteem in the world for him. It somehow made him believe he could be the man she thought he was.

Over a meal of chicken, potatoes, and greens, he told her of the sweet elderly couple and of the young mother with the newborn baby who had come for photographs that day. And she told him of her mishaps with a cake—which would most certainly *not* be on the table that evening.

After eating, they retired to the parlor where Nate struck up a low blaze, just warm enough to ward off the slight chill that came with nightfall. Ruthann settled in with sewing a set of curtains she hoped to hang over the window in the bedroom, and Nate turned the pages of a book without reading it. It was hard to concentrate with Ruthann sitting nearby. He found himself wanting to hear the sound of her voice instead. And so he thought he'd ask her about something that had been on his mind lately.

"Has Norah been to visit Jeremy?" The thought of his old friend wasting away in the prison just outside of town sat heavy with him. And Stuart hadn't said much on the subject, changing it to a different topic entirely when Nate had brought it up. Something about it seemed to bother Stuart greatly, and so Nate had chosen not to press him.

"She hasn't," Ruthann said, setting her sewing on her lap. "But not by her own choice."

"Her parents?"

Ruthann nodded. "I believe her when she says Jeremy wasn't guilty. He'd made some poor decisions, but I never thought him the sort to . . . well."

Murder. She needn't say the word aloud for Nate to understand. "It came as a shock to me, to be honest. I take it Stuart hasn't visited?"

Ruthann raised her eyebrows, as if she was surprised Nate was asking her instead of her brother. "He has not." She sighed. "He hasn't spoken of it, but I believe he and Jeremy had a falling out before everything happened. He didn't much get along with Jeremy's new friends."

Nate pressed his lips together. It would make sense, given Stuart's strong sense of right and wrong. If Jeremy had been treading on the wrong side of the law, Stuart would have considered their friendship over.

"Nate?" Ruthann asked quietly. "Are you wanting to pay a visit to him?"

Nate drew in a breath. Was he? "Yes. But not yet." It seemed wise to gather more information about the situation before potentially involving himself. "I have enough happening here right now." He smiled at Ruthann, knowing he'd see one in return.

She didn't disappoint him, and the sweet grin she gave him warmed the room better than the fire before them ever could have. She was so incredibly beautiful, with glowing skin and that smile that could disarm any man who still had life within him.

As if it had a mind of its own, his hand reached out to take hers. Just like at church and by the river, she accepted the gesture of affection. What that meant, he almost didn't dare contemplate. And how Stuart might feel about it . . . he certainly didn't care to entertain that thought right now.

But now the other question that had been gnawing at the edges of his mind since he first found her helping Mr. McGregor get home resurfaced. Emboldened by the way she'd answered his queries about Jeremy and how she allowed him to take her hand, he decided to voice it aloud.

"How is it you never married? Before now, of course."

She blushed at his question, and Nate tried not to think too much about how that seemed to make her even prettier.

"Well, I suppose there are a few answers to that question," she said, her eyes on the fire.

"Surely you had suitors?" He couldn't imagine her *not* having gentlemen interested.

"I did." She looked at him now, those clear blue eyes full of curiosity.

He wondered at that a moment, until the reason for the way she looked at him walloped him upside the head.

This was the most personal question he'd ever asked her.

Well, perhaps not the *most* personal. He wanted to cringe at some of the things he'd likely said to her when they were younger. But now, as a grown man—and one who'd mostly kept his thoughts to himself since his return—this was certainly the most intrusive sort of question he'd asked.

"I'm sorry. You don't have to answer that."

"It's all right." She smiled again. "It's only that you caught me by surprise."

Nate stiffened a little. It *was* out of character for him to ask so many questions, or, for that matter, speak so much. He hadn't wanted to, not for years. His mind couldn't piece together how to conduct a regular, innocuous conversation when so many horrors played through his head.

But there was something about Ruthann that made him feel . . . light. The awful things he'd seen were still there, but they felt further away. As if it had become harder for them to touch his life here, with Ruthann.

He swallowed, trying not to feel self-conscious about it all, and raised his eyebrows as if there were nothing else on his mind other than Ruthann and her previous suitors. "Well?"

"Well," she repeated, her sewing forgotten now. "I was fortunate to have more than one gentleman come to visit me."

An irrational, intense dislike of every single one of those men shot through Nate.

"They were all decent and kind men. Perfect for any woman, but not for me." She drew in a deep breath and looked at their intertwined hands.

That piqued his curiosity. "Why is that?"

"Not a one of them quite measured up."

"Measured up?" He turned the words over in his mind, trying to discern their meaning. "To what? Or whom?"

She raised her eyes then, capturing his immediately. When she spoke, her voice was but a whisper. "To you."

Chapter Thirteen

THE FOLLOWING DAY FOUND Ruthann scrubbing linens with more gusto than she could have ever imagined she'd pour into routine washing. And yet the constant back-and-forth motion and the ache in her arms helped ease her mind.

Since the night before, she'd been plagued by thoughts that swung wider than a clock pendulum. First, she would be relieved that she'd finally confessed her true feelings to Nate. The next moment, embarrassment took over, and she could hardly believe she'd bared a corner of her soul in that way—particularly since Nate hadn't responded in kind.

In fact, he'd abruptly ended the evening soon after and had barely said a word to her at breakfast that morning.

But she'd told him. And honesty was good . . . wasn't it?

Ruthann didn't know. It was all so confusing. She only wished she knew his thoughts, but Nate had folded up like a stubborn child, reverting right back to the man he'd been when they wed. And for a brief moment last night, things had felt so very normal. As if no time had passed, as if Nate had never left, as if his time away hadn't changed him at all.

It was wishful thinking to imagine him that joyful, open, carefree boy again. Ruthann knew that. But for the tiniest of moments last night, it had certainly felt that way. Perhaps that's why she'd been moved to confess why no other man had caught her attention.

She set aside the bedsheet before she scrubbed a hole into it. At least it was out in the open now. She hadn't asked him to reconsider the plans for annulment, and she certainly hadn't confessed love . . . but it was only natural that both of those thoughts must have crossed Nate's mind by now. Especially considering how quickly he'd withdrawn.

What if he doesn't feel the same? Ruthann shoved down that awful thought, taking up another linen and giving it a vigorous scrubbing against the washboard. He must feel something for her. A man didn't ask such prying questions or take a lady's hand unless he did.

Right?

"Ruthann."

She turned at the sound of his voice, and there he stood, cutting a striking figure in his black suit with that devil-may-care dark hair and those eyes that seemed to see right through her. No wonder Sissy Flagler had taken one look at him and decided to make him her mark. He was easily the best looking man in town, a fact Ruthann had known since she'd been old enough to think about such things.

"Yes," she said, pushing all her wild thoughts away and dropping the bedsheet.

"Might I ask for your help?" The words came out somewhat awkwardly, as if he'd never asked for help in his life.

Curiosity aroused, Ruthann stood. "In your studio?" He had a family scheduled for photographs this morning, if she remembered correctly. The Robinsons, who had, Ruthann believed, somewhere around eight young children. Or was it nine?

"Yes." A squeal sounded from inside, and Nate glanced briefly behind him before turning his attention to Ruthann again. "It's . . . ah . . . Well, it's difficult to ensure that all the children remain seated and still long enough for the image to expose."

Ruthann smiled at the thought of Nate attempting to convince a horde of little ones to remain perfectly still. Their parents certainly couldn't do it if they were in the photograph too. "I'm happy to help, but I'm in a work dress." She gestured at her water-splattered calico and apron.

Nate shook his head. "It doesn't matter."

He must be desperate, Ruthann thought. He was so careful with the way he presented himself each day that she assumed he'd wish the same of her if she was to help.

"Let me at least unpin my apron." She made quick work of it, leaving the garment draped over the rail on the back porch.

Inside, the younger children ran with wild abandon around the studio. Nate uprighted a small table that had been knocked over while Ruthann assessed the situation. The children's mother raised her hands and gestured at them to reassemble for the photograph while the oldest son scooped up a toddler who was pulling on Nate's pant leg.

"Children!" Mrs. Robinson's voice was commanding and yet gentle at the same time. Each child dutifully found his or her place as she took a baby from her husband's arms. All was well as Nate stood behind the camera again, but it wasn't long before Ruthann saw what had caused him such trouble. It wasn't that the children were ill-behaved; they simply couldn't stay in the same place without fidgeting. One of the boys elbowed his little sister, who started to cry, while another of the girls began to twist the long curls that hung down her back. Two of the older boys changed places, and to top it off, the baby began to fuss.

"I have an idea!" Ruthann announced loudly.

The children ceased moving immediately, and both parents looked at her in grateful hope.

"Let's play a game." She withdrew a penny from her pocket. It was one of a handful she'd failed to remove after a trip to Hill's General Store two days before, and now she was thankful for her absence of mind.

The children blinked at the shiny penny.

"Who would like this penny?" she asked.

Every single one of the children, with the exception of the baby, of course, raised a hand—even the toddler who Ruthann suspected didn't know what a penny was. But if his siblings wanted it, it made sense that he would too.

"Only one of you can win the coin," she said in a hushed voice. "But there are rules to this game."

They all leaned forward just slightly to hear her.

"First, you must stand up straight."

Each child did exactly that.

Ruthann nodded to Nate, who took the cue and bent his head behind the camera. "Secondly, you must remain absolutely still until I say otherwise."

They froze into place.

"And finally, you mustn't make a peep." She laid a finger against her lips.

It worked like a charm. Ruthann nodded at them every few minutes while she kept the penny out. Every single one of them remained as still as they could. Even the littlest ones tried not to squirm. Ruthann was so proud of them and gave them an encouraging smile as the time wound down.

When the right amount of time elapsed, Nate said, "I believe we have it."

Both Mr. and Mrs. Robinson sighed in relief as the children let out pent-up shrieks of delight and immediately began moving again.

"Which one of us gets the penny, Mrs. Harper?" one of the girls asked.

Ruthann smiled, partially in response to the girl's eagerness and partially from hearing herself referred to as *Mrs. Harper*. While Nate talked with Mr. and Mrs. Robinson, the children crowded around Ruthann.

"Hmm," Ruthann said, resting a finger against the side of her mouth as she considered each child. "You were all very good at this game."

"Don't give it to Tommy. He pinched me." One of the little boys looked ruefully at his brother.

Ruthann hid a smile behind her hand. "Well, I think in this situation, I'll have to change the rules just a little bit."

Among cries of "That isn't fair!" and "Why can't I win the penny?" Ruthann drew four more pennies from her pocket and presented all five coins to the eldest child, a boy of about twelve.

"Each of you deserves the penny, and so I'll entrust your brother to use this money to purchase a treat that you may all share evenly."

The boy nodded seriously and placed the coins in his pocket while his siblings chattered happily and thanked Ruthann.

"I still don't think Tommy should get any." The boy who'd been pinched crossed his arms and glared at the one Ruthann assumed was Tommy.

"He stayed as still as the rest of you, so in this case, I say that Tommy also deserves to share in the treat," Ruthann said.

The littler one didn't look appeased—at least until the eldest began talking about whether they should purchase peppermints or chocolates.

After the Robinsons left, Nate turned to Ruthann, who was busying herself with straightening the lace on the little end table. "Thank you. I don't know what I would have done without your help."

"You're welcome. I have to admit that I enjoyed it. They're sweet children, and I'm sure their photograph will be very good."

"I hope so." Nate frowned a moment. "I can't imagine having to do all of that over again."

"They are a handful," Ruthann admitted. She stepped around the table to where Nate was pulling the settee to an angle. "But I do love children, and I always wished I'd been part of a family that large."

"As did I." He glanced at her as he stepped back to assess the scene before them. "But mostly because being the only child meant I drew all of my mother's attention—which wasn't always for the best."

Ruthann laughed. "Well, I had a brother who was always in significantly more trouble than I could ever find, so I suppose

I had it much easier. I do hope to have a large family someday, though."

She didn't realize what she'd said until the words were out of her mouth and Nate had caught her gaze with his. Did he think she wanted a large family with *him*?

She did, of course. But given that she'd only just admitted her longstanding feelings for him last night, it seemed awfully soon to start discussing how many children she wished to have. Especially considering how he hadn't exactly reciprocated her feelings.

Ruthann clutched her fingers into her palms and prayed she hadn't scared him even further away. God appeared to be listening, because instead of closing her out and retreating as he'd done last night, Nate simply held her gaze.

It was impossible to see what he was thinking. But he didn't look away, and he didn't get that look in his eyes that meant he was withdrawing back into himself.

"I imagine you will be an excellent mother," he finally said, and Ruthann thought her heart would stop.

Yes, she hoped for more. A confession that he would like her to be his children's mother, for instance. But he was still here, with her, looking at her, *seeing* her, and that was enough.

"Would you like me to help with anything else?" she asked as she took a step forward.

But before he could answer, her toe caught the edge of the rug and she began to fall forward. Ruthann gave a little cry. Instinctively, she reached out her hands to break the fall—but found them pressed against Nate's chest instead of the floor.

He'd caught her.

And now, here she was, in his arms. Her face burned and she moved to extract herself, but he must have thought she'd lost her balance again, because his arms tightened around her.

And all she could do was look up—right into his face, which was so close she could feel his breath against her skin.

It was like every dream she'd had of him since the moment they'd shared six years before. But instead of being just an image in her mind, this was real.

He was close enough to kiss her.

Chapter Fourteen

HOLDING RUTHANN WAS everything Nate had dreamed it would be. She was soft and warm in his arms, her body leaning against his from where he'd broken her fall, his strength holding her up, and her sweet, flushed face tilted toward him.

She blinked, those gorgeous blue eyes finally seeming to take in what had happened. Her cheeks went scarlet, and all he wanted to do was press his lips against hers. It would be easy. In just a fraction of a second he could dip his head and taste her sweet kiss again, the way he had all those years ago.

The thought was like a roaring fire in his mind, blocking out all other sound and presence around him. It was only Ruthann and himself. Nothing else mattered.

Her eyes fluttered shut, almost as if she expected him to kiss her. The fire grew, and his mind spun.

They *were* married, weren't they?

Stuart would never need to know. It would be only one kiss. Didn't he deserve some sliver of happiness after all he'd experienced?

Stifling a groan, Nate closed his eyes. He couldn't do this, could he?

He *could*.

He opened his eyes again. She was still there, an angel in his arms. She didn't push him away. What was it she'd said last night? That no other man had ever measured up to him. To *him*.

How he'd dreamed of hearing her say such a thing. It had caught him entirely by surprise, and the guilt—oh, the guilt was all-consuming.

He'd been the reason she had never married.

And the way she stayed so still in his arms now, the trusting way she leaned against him, it was as if she wanted him to kiss her.

Ruthann, his wife. *His* wife.

And suddenly, he didn't care about anything but her and how right it felt to hold her in his arms. He moved closer to her lips and—

The front door opened, and with it came Stuart's voice. "Nate! Are you here?"

Nate jumped away from Ruthann as if she were made of the very fire that had been consuming his mind. She appeared dazed as he let go, and she grabbed on to the arm of the settee as if to steady herself. Nate whirled around, just as Stuart stepped through the doorway.

"I'm sorry, am I interrupting? Do you have customers?" Stuart's eyes searched the room, and, upon finding no one else present, his gaze returned to Nate and Ruthann.

Nate tugged uncomfortably at the hem of his jacket while Ruthann's face was as red as a late-summer tomato.

"Stuart, hello," she said, her soft voice a bit strangled. "I'm afraid I must get back to the washing."

And with that, she disappeared from the studio, leaving Nate to contend with his friend alone. As he should, considering he was the one who had promised Stuart he'd keep a friendly distance between himself and Ruthann.

Stuart looked at him with a confused expression, as if he hadn't seen anything Nate had done. And perhaps he hadn't. He had, after all, asked if there were customers present.

"Is everything all right?" Stuart finally asked. "Ruthann left so quickly. Did you argue?"

Nate drew in a breath, thanking God that Stuart suspected the utter opposite of what had actually happened. "Oh, no. We were simply . . . rearranging the studio." It wasn't a lie, not exactly. They had, after all, been straightening what the Robinson children had rearranged on their own.

"Ah. Well, it looks nice." Stuart gave the settee a quick, uninterested glance. He tucked his hands into his trouser pockets. "I don't suppose you've heard from Miss Flagler lately?"

Nate shook his head. "She came by shortly after we married, but not since then."

"Well, it appears she's taken up with someone new. No one seems to know the man, but she's been seen more than once in public with him."

Never had any news sounded like such music to Nate's ears. "That sounds promising."

Stuart nodded. "So it seems. You may not have to remain married much longer."

Nate forced his expression to remain neutral. It was what he wanted, wasn't it? To annul this marriage as soon as possible? To set Ruthann free to find a real union?

But if that was so, why did the reminder sit so poorly with him?

"I need to get back to work, as I'm sure you do too," Stuart said.

"Indeed." It was all Nate could seem to say.

As he bid goodbye to Stuart, he reminded himself that his friend had no reason to suspect Nate's true feelings. Which was for the best.

And yet it felt so *wrong*.

All those years he'd yearned to see Ruthann again, she'd felt the same way about him. How had he never guessed?

Because she's too good for you, that voice in the back of his mind reminded him as he crossed the studio to retrieve the plate from his camera.

It was true. She'd always been too good for him. She came from a respected family, not wealthy, but comfortable. And then there was him—growing up in what amounted to a shack, clean thanks to his mother who'd wanted so much more for them, but still poor. If only he'd known then how truly rich he was with a loving mother and his own, true self intact.

He'd lost himself since then, and if it was possible, he deserved Ruthann even less now than he did six years ago.

Yet it didn't seem to matter to her. She didn't complain when the memories forced him to close himself away, to withdraw to the quiet, to be alone while his mind tried to settle. He wasn't at all the man he used to be, and Ruthann seemed untroubled by that. In fact, she appeared to be entirely understanding.

Of course, she didn't know everything. And he would never tell her. Some horrors ought to be forgotten forever.

But he was slowly rebuilding a life here. And if he could do that, perhaps he could also rebuild himself as a person, push those old memories away for good. Maybe he could become the man Ruthann deserved.

The thought made him smile as he entered the darkroom.

What would it be like to be married to Ruthann—*truly* married—forever?

Chapter Fifteen

WHEN RUTHANN LEFT NORAH'S, the sky had turned cloudy and summer seemed to have gone with the sun. Most of the town, save for one brave soul who stood outside the home across the road, had gone inside to warm fires and a good roof.

Ruthann drew the shawl Norah had lent her closer around herself as she stepped down to the street. The wind picked up and sliced straight through the knit shawl. Ruthann shivered. Perhaps she ought to have waited for Norah's father to fetch their carriage. It had seemed silly, though, when she'd considered it while sitting inside her friend's cozy home, particularly since it wasn't all that far of a walk back to the studio.

Well, the only thing to do now was continue on. If she walked quickly, she would make it back home in no time at all.

Ruthann ducked her head against a strong gust and kept going, one foot in front of the other. If it began to rain, she could always duck into one of the shops or eateries that sat between here and the studio.

Heartened by that thought, she continued on.

She was halfway home when she had the strangest feeling that she wasn't alone. *Don't be silly*, she told herself. It was the middle of town, after all. Of course it made sense that others would be out.

Except they weren't, not in this weather.

Her heart beating faster, Ruthann turned her head slightly. Not a soul was across the road. There was no one in front of her. Saying a quick prayer, she glanced behind her.

A man followed her at a close distance. And, unless she was mistaken, it was the same man she'd seen across the street when she left Norah's house.

Perhaps he was simply headed elsewhere too. But as she passed two boardinghouses, a diner, the general store, and the jeweler's, he continued behind her.

And he was growing closer.

Something was wrong. Ruthann knew it as well as she knew her own face in the mirror.

She walked even more quickly. It wasn't that far now to the studio. She'd slip inside and lock the door before he could catch up with her.

She glanced back over her shoulder, needing to see him and yet hoping he didn't notice that she knew he was there. He was gaining distance and growing closer to her.

The town post office was just ahead. She could go inside there. The man surely wouldn't follow her. And if he waited outside, Mr. Doyle or one of his assistants would escort her home or fetch the sheriff.

Another gust of wind grabbed hold of the ends of Norah's shawl, and Ruthann reached out to catch it before it flew away. But just as she clutched on to it, she felt a tug on it from the other side.

As she turned to see what it had caught on, the shawl wrapped around her like a cocoon. Her eyes found the source of the pull, and it wasn't a tree branch or wayward piece of lumber.

It was the man who'd been following her.

"Let go!" Ruthann twisted to pull away, but the man was too strong for her. He propelled her around the side of the gunsmith's, next to the post office. Ruthann fought and turned back and forth, finally ducking low enough to let the shawl come over her head.

The movement freed her left side, and with just another twist, the shawl would be off completely—and she could run.

But the man must have seen the possibility too. He reached out and grabbed hold of her arm, letting the shawl fall to the ground.

Her heart in her throat, Ruthann felt a scream rising inside. Just as she opened her mouth to let it out, the man pushed her against the side of the building and slapped a gloved hand over her open mouth.

She pushed against him, but it was like pressing against a wall. The man stared at her a moment, his eyes, a green-gray, searching her face. He was young, perhaps around her age, with dark blond hair, and he stood as straight as a tree. All she could think was that she should have known him after spending her entire life in Cañon City. Then he spoke.

"Mrs. Harper," he said in a raspy voice.

Ruthann stilled. Whoever he was, he knew her. Yet she didn't know him. The thought was unnerving.

"I've a message for your husband. Tell him he ought not to go taking advantage of women, unless he wishes everyone to know what sort of man he really is."

His words made no sense to Ruthann at all. Taking advantage of women? Her mind raced, but the only thing that came to mind was Sissy. Did this man actually believe what she'd said? And what did he care about it?

"Did you hear me?" His face was closer to hers now, his breath unbearably warm against her wind-chilled face and his fingers digging into her arm. He bore a scar on his cheek that she couldn't seem to take her eyes from.

Ruthann nodded quickly.

"You'll give him the message?"

She nodded again. Anything to make him let her go.

"Good. I hope I don't need to find you again. But I will if I have to." And with that, he dropped his hands from both her face and her arm and was gone.

Ruthann didn't even see where he'd disappeared, instead sinking with relief to the ground. The skin around her mouth ached from where he'd pressed his hand, and her eyes stung with tears. The wind whipped around her, but she didn't care.

"Ruthann? Ruthann!"

She looked up to see Nate standing above her. He sunk down beside her, his hands instantly finding the muddy shawl and wrapping it around her shoulders. Ruthann shuddered, and he drew her to him.

"What's wrong? What happened?"

She bit her lip as she buried her face into his shoulder. He was so warm and steady, so very safe. Her entire body shuddered again as his arms wrapped around her.

"Can you stand?" he asked.

She nodded against him as she willed the tears to stop. Together, they rose from the ground, but he didn't let her go, not even a little, and Ruthann was grateful.

She didn't know how long they stood like that, against the wall of the gunsmith's building, his arms holding her tight to him. But finally, she tilted her head up.

"Can we go home?"

Without a word, he shifted his stance so that one arm wrapped around her shoulders, and he guided her the short way home.

Inside, he helped her up the stairs and onto the settee. Ruthann sunk into its welcome comfort as Nate sat next to her. He hadn't even bothered to remove his coat or hat.

"I'm all right," she finally said, although she wasn't entirely certain she believed it herself.

"You aren't," Nate said in a solemn voice. "What happened?"

Ruthann glanced up at him. Those dark eyes, which normally held so much behind them, looked fiercely protective now. And so she told him of the strange man, how he'd followed her and grabbed her, and what he'd said about Nate taking advantage of women.

"I don't know what it means," she said.

Nate shook his head. "Neither do I. I suppose he's referring to the incident with Miss Flagler. But how that would concern a stranger when her father was ready to burn down my entire life single-handedly, I don't know." He paused a moment. "Could he be the fellow who's courting Miss Flagler now?"

Ruthann thought back to the gossip she'd heard from various friends. "No. From what I've heard, he's a tall, thin fellow with very little hair. This man wasn't. He was . . ." She swallowed, remember how tightly he'd held on to her. "He was strong. His gloves were dirty. He looked like the sort of man who works hard for a living." She wondered if she'd ever forget the feel of those rough gloves pressed against her mouth. The leather had smelled of horseflesh and hay, scents Ruthann had never minded until now.

She shivered, and Nate drew off his coat. He set it around her shoulders and Ruthann smiled up at him gratefully. But instead of returning her smile, his eyes narrowed and he lifted a hand. Laying his thumb gently over the side of her mouth, he frowned. "Did he hit you?"

Ruthann shook her head ever so slightly, not wanting to dislodge his soothing touch. "No, only held his hand over my mouth."

"Far too hard," Nate said, and it sounded as if he were holding something behind the words, a dose of barely contained anger. He splayed his hand across her cheek, and warmth flooded her from head to toe. "He'd better hope I don't find him."

Ruthann reached up and clasped her hand around his arm. "Please don't do anything foolish." She swallowed, remembering the last part of the man's threat, which she hadn't told Nate about yet. "There is one more thing."

"Yes?" His thumb moved again, gently, protectively, over her cheekbone, and Ruthann felt her thoughts slipping away.

Unless he wishes everyone to know what sort of man he really is. What did that mean? It felt like some sort of imagined slight on Nate's character. Except Nate had no terrible flaws.

He was good. He was kind. He was perfect.

"Nothing important," she said, her voice coming in a wisp as his other hand gently cupped the opposite side of her face.

"I won't let anyone hurt you." His eyes were all fire and warmth with no trace of that haunted look she'd seen so often since he'd come back. They pinned her into place, and Ruthann couldn't have moved if she wanted to.

She certainly didn't want to.

For one breathless second, she held his gaze. How many times had she imagined a moment like this in her dreams? And now here they were—in anything but a dream. She raised a hand and laid it on his arm, just to remind herself of how very real this was.

And in that moment, as her fingers closed around his arm, he leaned down and kissed her.

Ruthann forgot how to breathe. She held on to his arm for dear life as his lips gently pressed against hers. They were soft and careful, as if he wasn't sure how she felt about his kiss.

She sighed with utter happiness. This was a dream, and it was coming true. Her heart felt as if it might burst, and all she wanted was to reach up and pull him even closer to her. She clutched his arm tighter and he stiffened.

And then it was over. Nate pulled away, and when Ruthann opened her eyes she found him watching her with a sort of reverent curiosity.

Was it possible that he'd pined for her the same way she'd thought of him for so many years? He hadn't said as much, yet the way he looked at her now . . . it was as if he'd satisfied some long-held desire in his heart.

He dropped his hands and took one of hers between them. She yearned to hear him confess his love for her, and for half a moment, with the way he held her gaze, she thought he might. But then he sighed, and his jaw set, and the moment passed.

"I believe you need a happy distraction," he said.

Ruthann thought his kiss was distraction enough. Her face went warm at the thought.

"One of the other churches on Macon Avenue—the one where we married—is holding a dance Saturday evening. Would you like to go?" he asked.

Ruthann couldn't have been more surprised than if he'd asked her if she wanted to float away in a hot air balloon. The Nate of six years ago would have loved a dance. She never would have thought the Nate of today would be interested. She smiled broadly, picturing him whirling her about the dance floor. "I would."

Turning more serious, he brushed his knuckles against her cheek again. "I don't want you to worry about that man. I'll find out who he is. And I'll see to it he never bothers us again." He pulled his hand away and smiled. "Now how about you sit here and rest, and I find us something to eat?"

Ruthann bit her lip as Nate rose and left for the kitchen. She ought to have told him the rest of what that man had said, about Nate not being the man everyone thought he was. But it was such an odd statement, and she truly wondered if it was an empty threat, something made up to scare her.

None of it made much sense, and the last thing she wanted to do was send Nate into a spiral of worry. He finally seemed to have put some distance between himself and whatever had happened to him in the past.

Ruthann wouldn't ruin that. All she wanted was for him to be happy. She would keep that man's words to herself, unless she found a good reason not to.

Chapter Sixteen

THERE WERE MORE PEOPLE crowded into the grassy area behind the church than Nate had been around in a long time. While Ruthann stepped forward, he hung back, trying to steady his breathing.

"Are you all right?" Ruthann asked, her fingers still clasped in his.

The sweet concern in her eyes was enough to banish any fears that lingered. There was no reason to be anxious. After all, this was where he'd grown up. He knew most of the people present, even if he hadn't seen many of them for years. The familiar faces made it easier to breathe, but mostly it was Ruthann's gentle strength that made him nod and step forward to stand beside her.

Ruthann scanned the crowd, some of whom were dancing along to the lively band, while others stood about talking or visited the tables laden with lemonade and other treats.

Nate spotted Stuart, standing off to the side with Norah. He raised his hand to greet them.

"Shall we join them?" Ruthann asked, casting a joyful smile up at Nate.

His heart soared at just that simple look. With Ruthann at his side, it seemed there was nothing else for which he could want.

He realized a second too late that he was still grasping Ruthann's hand. Stuart's smile flickered into a frown. Nate squeezed Ruthann's hand before letting go.

"Your brother," he whispered as an explanation.

"Yes," she said, although her voice was uncertain.

Nate glanced down at her, but her attention was already on Stuart and Norah, who had a slight flush to her cheeks.

Ruthann and Norah embraced, as Stuart eyed Nate with a curious look. But whatever was on his mind—and Nate suspected it was him and Ruthann—he didn't get to voice it, because Norah gasped.

"What is it?" Ruthann asked.

"Sissy is here," Norah replied. "With that gentleman she's been seen with."

Nate followed Norah's gaze, and certain enough, Miss Flagler was dancing with a man Nate didn't recognize. He was taller, with a balding pate that was evident even beneath his hat. "That looks like good news to me."

"It does indeed," Stuart said. "And I believe it calls for celebration. Would you care to dance?" He held out an arm to Norah, who gave a merry laugh and took it.

As Stuart led Norah to the dance floor, Nate glanced at Ruthann, who watched her friend and her brother with her head tilted.

"You don't see that man who grabbed you here anywhere?" It was a concern that had been on his mind, although he could hardly picture someone of that nature showing his face at a church dance.

What he hadn't mentioned to Ruthann was how unnerving it was that the fellow apparently didn't mind the possibility of Ruthann recognizing him. If he had, he would have covered his face in some way.

She looked around the crowd now and shook her head. "Thankfully, no."

"In that case, Mrs. Harper, would you care for a dance?" He extended a hand to her.

Ruthann's face brightened and she gave him the smile he'd hoped for. "I would, Mr. Harper. Thank you."

The band played a lively fiddle tune that required a fast pace. Nate whirled Ruthann around the makeshift dance floor. She laughed when he twirled her about a corner, and he thought there was no better sound in the world.

Making Ruthann happy made him happier than he'd ever thought possible.

Out here, with her in his arms, with a smile on her face that was only for him, and with all the trust in the world, he felt so very . . . whole. The memories of the past were still there, but they were just that—*memories*. Far away, cloudy, and unable to hurt him.

When the fiddler stopped and took a bow, and the rest of the band picked up a slower melody designed to allow the dancers to catch their breath, Ruthann looked up at him.

"I like seeing you smile," she said as they settled into a slower dance.

"Oh, do I frown too often?" He was joking, and yet he knew it was true.

"No, I wouldn't say that. It's more that it seems as if much of the time, you have something heavy weighing on your mind."

Nate swallowed. "I suppose that's true. I also didn't have much to smile about before."

"Before?" She raised her eyebrows, daring him to finish the thought.

And that made him smile again. "You've given me much to be happy about, Ruthann."

He might have told her that she was the most beautiful woman in the world, or that they were suddenly wealthier than Rockefellers, with the way she beamed at him.

"I am glad for that," she said. "Although I hope you'll trust me with your concerns and your less joyous experiences too."

Thankfully, the band struck up another raucous tune, allowing Nate to avoid responding. He suspected she meant sharing what had changed him so much, and he wasn't ready for that.

He didn't think he'd ever be ready to share that memory with anyone. It was much better tucked away where it could do no more damage.

They passed Stuart, who was now dancing with another young lady. And if Nate wasn't mistaken, he would have said his friend's expression was cautious when he saw Nate—as if he suspected there might be something more going on between Nate and Ruthann than the simple plan they'd cooked up a few weeks ago.

And he'd be right.

But as much as Nate didn't wish to anger or disappoint his oldest friend, he couldn't imagine not having Ruthann by his side. There had to be a way they could assuage Stuart's concerns. And surely Stuart would understand if they each spoke with him.

Although that would mean Nate was willing to remain married.

He almost stopped in his tracks. Ruthann glanced at him in concern, and Nate gave her a reassuring smile.

Did he *want* to remain married?

Ruthann seemed to believe he did. And Nate almost dared believe that she enjoyed being with him. That her trust in him was soundly placed, and that he truly was the man she'd been waiting for.

Could he be?

Was he?

In that moment, with Ruthann clutching his hands and looking up at him, with the sun sinking into a brilliant array of colors, and with the town he'd known and loved all around him, he thought that the answer was yes.

He could be brave enough to be the sort of man who was a good husband, not one who was shackled to the horrors of the past. The sort of man Ruthann deserved.

So long as the past stayed in the past, the future was a brilliant, wide-open opportunity full of hope and happiness and—Nate prayed—love.

Chapter Seventeen

WHEN RUTHANN REACHED Hill's General Store, she breathed a sigh of relief. In all her years in Cañon City, she never thought she'd feel a degree of terror simply walking through the main part of town in the afternoon. And yet, she never thought she'd be accosted by a stranger in the middle of the day either.

Thankfully, there had been no sign of that man. It was as if he'd arrived and fled town the same day, and Ruthann could only hope that was true. In the meantime, after many conversations during which she'd had to convince Nate that it was perfectly safe for her to walk around town alone, she held her breath and stayed watchful whenever she left home.

It was bustling inside the store, filled with people Ruthann knew or at least recognized, which was reassuring. Jasper Hill stood behind the counter, filling an order for Penny Young, the sheriff's wife. Ruthann said hello to Penny, who asked if she'd seen any more trouble.

"I haven't, thankfully. I hope that man has left town."

"Well, if he has any sense whatsoever, he has," Penny replied as Mr. Hill slid a wrapped parcel across the counter toward her. "How odd it is not to see Molly behind the counter," she said to Jasper as she took the package.

"Is she enjoying Denver?" Ruthann added.

"She is," Mr. Hill said, although he made a pained face with the reply. Ruthann dared not ask whether it was because he didn't have his sister's help or because he disapproved of her summer visit to Denver, where his mother had already told Ruthann that Molly was hoping to meet a husband. She glanced at Penny, who raised her eyebrows, but who also—wisely—said not a word.

Penny thanked Mr. Hill and laid a hand on Ruthann's arm. "If you see that man again, or feel frightened, all you need to do is tell Ben or myself. He can ensure someone watches the photography studio, as he did for this store last summer."

"Thank you," Ruthann said. She hoped her situation wouldn't escalate to the fear Mr. Hill and his wife Grace felt when Grace had inadvertently interfered with some outlaws' escape plans from the Territorial Prison on the edge of town.

After Penny left, Ruthann peeked into Grace Hill's dress shop at the rear of the store. But Grace was busy showing a customer some fabric, and so Ruthann attended to the reason she'd come into the store in the first place.

The men's pocket watches were arrayed in a pleasing fashion atop the end of the counter. Nate's pocket watch was entirely unreliable, and as patient as he was with it, Ruthann thought it might be nice to purchase him a new one—particularly since his birthday was today. He hadn't mentioned it to her at all, but there were things a woman never forgot about the man she'd thought of daily since she was sixteen years old.

With Mr. Hill's assistance, she chose a simple but masculine watch. He wrapped it for her and agreed to hold it at the counter while she completed her shopping. There were only a couple of other items Ruthann needed, but she took her time walking around the store. Perusing the items in stock at the general store was one of her favorite things to do. As she walked and admired the various items for sale, she thought on the cake she'd prepared and the meal full of Nate's favorite foods. She hoped he'd be surprised and happy with it.

"That one is pretty, but it doesn't hold a candle to what can be purchased in New York. If you're so lucky as to visit, anyway. I purchased several when I went last year for Ada Boone's wedding."

Ruthann looked up in surprise. Sissy stood right next to her. Where she'd come from, Ruthann couldn't imagine, but she quickly set down the gold and pearl hatpin she'd been admiring.

"How are you, Sissy?" she asked, ignoring the other woman's slight. "It was wonderful to see you having such a good time at the church dance."

"Oh, yes, Paul and I thoroughly enjoyed ourselves, although I wish this town would invest in a proper ballroom for such dances." She paused, her eyes narrowing just slightly. "It appears you and Mr. Harper had a fine evening too."

"We did," Ruthann said cautiously. Sissy was smiling again, but it felt forced. Was Ruthann imagining it? She had to be. Why in the world would Sissy be jealous when she had a new beau?

"I'm sorry I didn't come to say hello. I'm afraid I was so caught up in the fun that I hardly noticed who was there and who was not." Sissy giggled, and the sound set Ruthann on edge. She couldn't help but hope Sissy married this new beau of hers and they both went back East, to New York or anywhere far from Cañon City.

"It's quite all right." Ruthann gave Sissy an encouraging smile. She much preferred Sissy be infatuated with her new beau than remember how Nate had rejected her. "I haven't met your fellow, but I noticed more than one lady looking his way."

Sissy lifted her chin, the corners of her mouth rising at Ruthann's words. Jealousy was something Sissy thrived upon, and Ruthann's statement had the exact effect she thought it would. "I'm not surprised. Paul is quite the catch."

Ruthann nodded along. "I'm very happy for you."

"Thank you. That means quite a lot." The way Sissy spoke the words indicated that it didn't mean much at all to her, but Ruthann suspected she was happy that so many people had noticed her with her beau.

Sissy reached out and picked up the hatpin Ruthann had laid back on the display shelf. She turned it over absentmindedly as she looked back up at Ruthann. "A friend of mine mentioned something that worried me. And I'd feel remiss if I didn't share it with you."

"Oh?" Ruthann couldn't imagine what Sissy's so-called friend might have said to her.

"Yes." Sissy pressed the sharp tip of the hatpin against her gloved finger, but she didn't take her eyes from Ruthann. "On several occasions, when you were occupied with others, he saw that Mr. Harper was watching Paul and me. I want to think it was because he was happy for us, but my experience with him makes me hesitate."

Ruthann blinked at her. Surely she couldn't still be *that* fixated on Nate.

"I know you don't wish to believe ill of your husband, but you also didn't see the way he looked at me when we were in the studio. Considering you were in the darkroom, right?"

Ruthann nodded. She'd been so thankful that she'd never had to tell that lie, but Sissy was forcing her into it now.

"Well." Sissy balanced the hatpin between her fingers as she gave Ruthann a troubled smile. "It was concerning, to say the least. But I thought he'd put it behind him when he married you, so I didn't worry about it any further—until now. I just thought you'd like to know. I'd hate to see Paul needing to confront him, after all. And I'd especially hate for the entire town to find out what sort of man he really is."

Sissy set the hatpin back on the shelf. "You should buy that if you like it."

But Ruthann's mind certainly wasn't on hatpins. *What sort of man he really is.* Those were the words the man who had grabbed her on the street had said. Could it be a coincidence? Or was Sissy spreading lies about Nate to strangers?

Dangerous strangers.

"I may. I haven't yet decided." Ruthann forced herself to keep a neutral expression. She needed a moment to think, to put the pieces together and see what made sense and what didn't. "Excuse me, Sissy, I need to be getting home."

Setting her unpurchased items on the nearest shelf, Ruthann retrieved her package from the counter and walked straight to the door, not daring to look back. She didn't want Sissy to know that she'd unsettled her at all.

"Oh, Ruthann?" Sissy called in the most unladylike manner across the store. "Do say hello to your husband for me."

Ruthann bit the inside of her cheek. Those words were to let everyone in the store present know that Sissy still believed she had some sort of hold over Nate. She didn't want him—that much was clear from her mooning over her new beau—but she seemed to wish he wanted her.

It's nothing, Ruthann told herself as she exited the store. Sissy wanted to believe that every man was madly in love with her, and when it became clear they weren't, she said such things to make herself feel better.

That was all it was. She'd likely hinted at misdeeds in Nate's past to make herself look like the better person, and if she'd told her beau, he'd likely mentioned the same to friends, such as the man who'd grabbed her by the gunsmith's.

Although why that man was so angry about it was baffling.

None of it made sense, but so long as he was gone from town, did it matter? She ought to think of good things, like Nate's more frequent smile, how he might react to the dinner she'd prepared especially for his birthday, his kiss . . .

That thought made her blush as she made her way down the street. She hurried home, thoughts of Sissy and the stranger from the street melting away like the snow in spring.

Chapter Eighteen

A KNOCK CAME AT THE studio door, and Nate hurried to answer it. It should be his last appointment of the day—his birthday. Word of his photographs had gotten around town, and he was starting to find himself busy for most of the day. It was exactly what he wanted. During the day, he could bury himself in the art of the camera and developing photographs, and in the evenings, he spent comfortable hours with Ruthann.

He'd kissed her since that first time, more than once, and each time it was as if a piece of him came back to life. As if he was slowly reclaiming the person he used to be.

And it was all because of Ruthann.

Nate pulled the door open—and stared.

The man on the other side, likely younger than Nate and wearing a uniform, looked back at him, confused. "Is this the photography studio?" He glanced up at the sign, uncertain.

"Yes." Nate's voice came out strangled. He stepped back and opened the door further, gesturing for the man to come inside. "I'll be— Excuse me a moment."

And without waiting for an answer, he turned and grabbed his camera to make the man think his sudden disappearance to the darkroom had something to do with his work. Inside the darkroom, he shut the door and leaned against it, closing his eyes against the darkness.

Breathe, Harper. It was easier in here, away from the uniform that Nate himself had worn for so many years. He hadn't seen it since he'd left the Dakota Territory. And seeing it now . . . the memories had come crashing around him like boulders during an avalanche. He couldn't control them, couldn't stop them, couldn't do anything except *remember*.

His breath shuddered in and out as he opened his eyes and stared into the black of the darkroom. The screams, the roar of gunfire, the blood, all of it slowly fell back to where he'd kept it since returning. Far away from his new life. Far away from Ruthann.

"Mr. Harper, sir?" The younger man's voice came from outside the door.

Nate swallowed and forced himself to stand up straight. Running a hand across his face, he paused and then opened the door. Everything was all right. This soldier simply wanted his photograph made for his family before he went away to join the Army. "I apologize. I had a plate I needed to remove immediately. Would you like to begin?"

The session moved along quickly, and after the man left, Nate locked the door and sat on the settee. He leaned back, utterly spent, as if he'd just run for miles instead of standing in one room and taking photographs.

And that was where Ruthann found him when she came downstairs.

"Nate? Are you well?" She sat beside him on the settee and tilted her head as she looked at him in concern. She held something clasped in her hands.

He raised his head, not wanting to worry her. "I'm fine. I apologize for not coming upstairs sooner. What have you got?" He nodded at her hands.

The corners of her lips raised in a sly smile. "Just a little something I thought you might like. It *is* your birthday, after all."

Nate blinked. He hadn't told her. Perhaps she'd spoken with Stuart. Or . . . she'd remembered. It was possible. After all, he knew hers like it was his own.

"I'm sorry, I remembered the day, and I thought you might like a small celebration. Just the two of us," she added quickly, for which he was thankful. He couldn't imagine summoning the energy he would need for a larger group of people right now, not after nearly succumbing to the memories less than an hour ago.

"Thank you," he said, meaning it from the bottom of his heart. "I didn't expect you to remember." He glanced at her hands again, curious.

She smiled and opened them to reveal a cornbread muffin. But it wasn't just any cornbread muffin; it was dotted with flecks of green.

"Peppers," he said, his stomach rumbling at the very thought.

"I remembered how much you liked that cornbread with the spicy peppers that Mama made sometimes." She held the muffin out to him.

Nate took it, nearly salivating as he bit into it. He closed his eyes. It was just as good as he remembered, but even better. Whether that was because it had been so long since he'd had one, or because Ruthann had perfected her mother's recipe, he didn't know. "I could eat ten more of these."

She laughed. "Well, there are eleven more upstairs. Along with chicken cooked with lemons, buttered mashed potatoes, and baked apples."

All of his favorite foods. It was a good thing he'd shoved the rest of the cornbread into his mouth, or his jaw would have been hanging open. He chewed and swallowed. "How did you know?" She couldn't remember all of that from their childhood.

She laughed, light and airy and leaving no room for the specters that had haunted him earlier. "I have my ways."

"Mmhmm." He couldn't imagine what those were beyond talking with her brother, who Nate could imagine giving her the information with a highly suspicious lift to his eyebrows.

He'd have to tell Stuart, sooner rather than later. They couldn't go on like this if he wasn't being honest with his oldest friend.

Ruthann stood and smoothed the pretty yellow skirt she wore before extending a hand to Nate. "Are you certain all is well? You looked absolutely exhausted before."

He took her hand and stood, relishing the simple feel of her fingers curling around his. She watched him with an open expression. She wanted to know his thoughts.

Nate drew in a breath. It wouldn't hurt to tell her some of it. In fact, getting it out of his head might help. But only a little. The rest didn't have a place here.

He shifted his hand so that his fingers encircled hers, reminding him that he was protective and strong. Not weak, not prone to succumbing to fear. And most certainly not a coward. All was well here.

"The last man who came for his photo, Francis Barrett?" He paused as Ruthann nodded in recognition. "He arrived in uniform, wanting a photo he could leave with his family before he left."

"Yes, I remember his mother saying he'd joined the Army," Ruthann said.

Nate let himself sink into the measured, warm tone of her voice. *All was well here.* "I didn't expect it—the uniform." He paused, expecting to see confusion in Ruthann's face. After all, why would a uniform worry a man so much? But she simply nodded, as if she completely understood. She couldn't, of course, but her openness heartened him, and he went on. "There were good parts about my time in the cavalry. And times I'd rather forget . . . but I can't. And seeing him in that uniform brought it all back to me."

"I'm sorry that happened," she said. "It must have been hard."

Nate's heart warmed, and all he wanted to do was take her into his arms and kiss her until he forgot all of it. He settled for pressing a strand of hair away from her face and behind her ear. "I'm fine now, I promise. It was momentary."

She nodded, and he hoped she believed him. He'd brushed it off as if it weren't nearly as terrible as it was. But he'd told the truth. He *was* fine right now, and he had been for a while—because of her. There was no need to resurrect the ghosts that had threatened him earlier. He'd put them all right back where they'd belonged and successfully taken the photograph his customer wanted.

"Then I believe a birthday celebration is in order," Ruthann said, smiling again. "Shall we?"

He stepped back, dropping her hand and gesturing toward the stairs. "I can hardly wait. I don't suppose you're hungry too?"

She laughed. "Don't you dare eat *all* of the food, Nathaniel Harper!"

"Then I suppose you'd better get upstairs and get some before I have at it."

She tossed a grin back at him before climbing the stairs. He came up slowly behind her, banishing the bad memories as he went and moving his thoughts toward better ones.

He would be just fine, so long as he could keep the past where it belonged, and his reaction to it in check.

That sad, trembling shell of a man belonged far away in the windswept Dakota Territory, against the shadows of the Black Hills. He wasn't that person anymore. Here, he was Nate Harper again, perfectly able to live a normal life. Capable of running his own business, protecting what was his, and—if he didn't lose a friend in the process and all went well—enjoying a family of his own.

The ghosts were just that. Ghosts. They couldn't hurt him here if he didn't let them.

Chapter Nineteen

THE HOUSES ON THE EDGE of town grew farther and farther apart until there was nothing but scrubby green growing up in the dirt here and there and, not too far away, the rise of the hills.

"I always thought I'd like to live out here," Norah said, shading her eyes against the sun as they looked out over the hills.

"On a ranch?" Ruthann couldn't picture her friend as a rancher's wife, cooking up big batches of food while fighting back the dust and dirt.

"Certainly not," Norah replied, and Ruthann laughed. "Just out here on the edge of town, where it's quiet and when you look out your back window, all you see is grass and trees and hills and birds. It's . . . peaceful."

Ruthann nodded. "It is. I don't know that I'd be comfortable so far from everyone, though."

Three children tumbled out the door of the last house before the town gave way to the wilderness, and Ruthann smiled at their antics. It *was* a good place for children to grow up. After all, she and Stuart had spent many an afternoon out past the town, climbing trees and playing along the river and rolling down hills.

"Imagine having such fun right outside your door rather than trudging through town to get to it," Norah said as if she read Ruthann's thoughts.

Ruthann glanced at her friend, who had a faraway look in her eye and a content smile. It was almost as if she were picturing just that sort of life. Ruthann bumped her friend gently on the arm. "Thinking of sharing that little house with anyone in particular?"

Norah's face colored. *Was* there someone Norah cared for? If so, she hadn't mentioned a word of it to Ruthann. She yearned to ask Norah for more, but bit her tongue. If Norah were pining after someone, she would tell her friend in due time. Ruthann only need be patient.

"Mmhmm," was all Norah said with a little smile playing upon her lips as she looked out toward the gently rising hills.

Ruthann followed her gaze. Movement in the distance caught her eye, and she squinted, trying to make out whether it was an animal, a person, or simply the rustle of vegetation in the breeze.

"Do you see that?" She pointed as it moved again.

After a few seconds, Norah nodded. "I do . . . It looks like people."

Ruthann squinted again. Norah was right. There were two people, and after a moment, they parted—one heading back up over the hill and the other, a man, returning toward town.

Norah took hold of Ruthann's arm. "Something about this feels odd."

Ruthann swallowed. Her friend was right. Why would this man be out past the edge of town meeting with someone else?

And where was the other man going without a horse? "Perhaps we should head back toward home."

Norah met her eyes in silent agreement, and they turned together and began to walk quickly. Ruthann glanced behind her. The man had grown closer, clearly walking at a faster clip than the two women. He had removed his hat, and the sun glinted off his hair, which appeared to be between blond and brown at this distance.

Ruthann turned back around and tried to force her mind away from the thought that had instantly surfaced upon seeing the man's hair. Many people had hair that color. In fact, it was similar to the shade that both Ruthann and Stuart bore. Simply having dark blond hair didn't mean this man was the same as the one who had grabbed her off the street. Besides, that man hadn't been seen in town since then.

Perhaps because he'd been out in the hills with that other man.

No, her mind was getting carried away now. At worst, the fellow behind them was a drifter. But it was more likely he was simply meeting a nearby rancher for business.

A rancher without a horse.

Ruthann couldn't ignore the panic rising inside her. Norah kept hold of her arm and they walked as fast as they could. The houses were growing closer together, although they had yet to reach the part of town that was dense enough for businesses.

She couldn't help but turn and look again.

The man had grown even closer. And worse, his eyes were fixed on them.

"It's him," Ruthann whispered. She was sure of it. Even without seeing the color of his eyes or being able to make out a scar on his face, she *knew* it was the man who had cornered her.

Norah looked at her in alarm, clearly understanding who it was that Ruthann meant. "Are you certain?"

Ruthann nodded, and Norah's hand tightened around her arm.

"Mrs. Williams lives just ahead. We could go there."

"No, we can't bring him to her home. She's a widow." Ruthann would never forgive herself if anything terrible happened.

"Then we must keep going." Norah took on a determined expression.

The first cross street—and with it, a smattering of businesses—was just ahead. If they could reach that area, at least there would be more people about. Unlike the day the man had found Ruthann, today was a lovely, bright, warm day, with plenty of folks outside to enjoy it.

He wouldn't dare do anything with so many others around.

And yet when Ruthann turned again, the man wasn't half a block away. How had he moved so quickly? It was most certainly him, there was no denying it at all now. That scar glinted pink in the sunlight, and his eyes remained on her and Norah.

"Norah—" But before Ruthann could continue, Norah pointed straight ahead and said, "Isn't that Nate?"

Ruthann turned to look ahead and—yes! It *was* Nate, just ahead and walking toward them.

She didn't care who heard her, or how unladylike it was to shout on the street. "Nate!" she yelled, her voice laced with terror.

He must have heard her urgency, because as the people around him turned to stare, Nate began to jog toward them.

When he reached the girls, Ruthann turned and pointed to the man who had stopped behind them. "It's him."

She didn't have to explain any further.

Without a word, Nate ran.

Chapter Twenty

SOMETHING PRIMAL AND angry arose in Nate the second his eyes landed on the scarred man who walked several feet behind Ruthann and Norah. Ruthann didn't need to explain; from the panic in her voice and Norah's wide eyes, it was evident that the man Ruthann pointed to was none other than the one who had grabbed her and had hauled her off the street.

Nate didn't think. He simply ran.

It took the other man a moment, but once he realized what Nate was doing, he ran too. Nate wanted to grab hold of the man, turn him around, and look him in the eye before he told him to stay away from his wife and this entire town. The man was armed, that was clear from the holster at his hip. And Nate was not, but that thought didn't hold him back.

Whether it was because he was taller and stronger or because of the sheer physical effort he'd exerted, Nate caught up to the man just before they reached the edge of town. Nearby, three children lurked outside the front of a house. Nate noticed them just as he reached forward and grabbed hold of the man's coat.

They tumbled to the ground. The blond man crawled forward, but Nate had the foresight to reach for the pistol at the man's hip. Yanking it from the holster, he stood at the same time and held it out.

The man backed up a few steps, his hands outstretched. "I didn't mean no harm."

Nate barely heard him. The pistol felt as heavy as a horse in his hands, the metal strangely warm. He hadn't held a gun since he'd left the Dakota Territory. Hadn't even looked at one. He'd tossed his pistols into the bottom of a carpetbag when he left, and that's where they still sat. Memories fought to burst into his mind, and he squeezed his hand around the grip to force them away.

He finally found words and ground them out. "What do you want with my wife?"

"Nothing. Like I said, I didn't mean anything by it at all."

"By what? Chasing her into town or grabbing her outside the gunsmith's?"

The man said nothing, his eyes drifting to his revolver in Nate's hand. Nate followed the man's gaze to see his own hand beginning to tremble. He raised his other hand to steady his grip.

Screaming. Blood . . . so much blood. A mother holding a wailing child. Men and women on the ground, not moving.

Nate bit down hard on the inside of his cheek. He couldn't let it in now. *Later.* He'd deal with the memories later.

But they didn't retreat. They crowded into his mind, forcing his aim to drop.

The blond man smiled, just barely, but he didn't lower his hands. "They said you were a coward."

Nate drew in a breath. That ought to anger him, make him lunge at the man or at least level his aim.

But it didn't. It couldn't—there was no room for it among the images that fought for dominance in his mind. *That baby crying. The mother hunched over her fallen husband. Men—his fellow soldiers—running around him while he stood perfectly still.*

Coward.

He wasn't, though. Somewhere deep in his mind, he knew that. It wasn't cowardice.

It was horror. Shock. Anger. Guilt.

A hundred different emotions, but not fear. Not cowardice.

How did he *know*?

"Did your pretty wife give you my warning?"

The man's words drew Nate's attention back to him.

"If you don't heed it, this entire town will know about you." And with that, the man dropped his hands and ran, leaving Nate standing in the road with his pistol.

Nate didn't chase him. He couldn't have. Instead, it was like every bit of life had left him, and he doubled over, his hands on his knees, still holding that man's pistol.

This entire town will know about you. Know about . . . what? And what did he say to Ruthann? She didn't mention a warning of any sort.

Nate drew in great gulps of air, and his heartbeat slowed. He stood again. Across the road, those same three children watched him.

"You all right, mister?" the oldest one asked.

Nate held up a hand to indicate he was. He didn't trust himself with words just yet. He had to get back to Ruthann and Norah before they began to worry.

One foot in front of the other, he walked, with that pistol hanging in his hand. It burned like hot coal. He wanted to drop it—and with it, drop all the memories it yanked back into his mind. And yet he couldn't simply leave it in the road.

"Nate!" Ruthann's voice, as soothing as cool cloth against a fever, came from just ahead.

He looked up to find her moving quickly toward him.

In no time, she'd reached him and had flung her arms around him. "You're all right, thank goodness. Norah went for the sheriff." She stood back, her hands still on his arms, and looked around him. "Is he gone?"

"Yes." Nate drug the word out.

The worry eased on Ruthann's face. "Where did you get—" She gestured at the pistol.

He shook his head, the words gone again. He'd been useless with it. And worse, that man *knew*. He'd taken a gamble and had run, because he knew Nate couldn't bring himself to pull the trigger.

Ruthann must have seen something in his face, because she said in a low voice, "Would you like me to take it?"

He did, and yet he didn't. He didn't want to hold the thing any longer. But what sort of man did that make him?

Ruthann gently eased it from his fingers, and Nate didn't say a word. The second it was gone, he thought the memories would retreat again.

But they didn't.

They still lurked at the edges of his mind, ready to jump out and destroy everything. Destroy *him*.

"Let's go home. The sheriff can meet us there." She wrapped an arm around his elbow as if she still trusted him to protect her.

They said you were a coward.

Was that what he was threatening to tell the town? But he wasn't a coward. Not now . . . and yet . . .

He couldn't have used that pistol if he'd needed to. He could hardly even hold the weapon without falling apart. Perhaps he hadn't been a coward then, but it sure seemed he was now.

What would he have done if the man hadn't left? If he'd gone after Ruthann again? He'd just stood there like a fool who'd never held a gun before. Useless and broken.

He had promised Ruthann that he would keep her safe. He'd promised Stuart.

But he couldn't protect her.

Nate glanced at her now, her eyes studying the way ahead of them, her arm wrapped securely around his, and that pistol safely held in her other hand. It was as if she was the one protecting him.

He was grateful, and ashamed.

She deserved so much better.

Chapter Twenty-one

"I'LL SEND SOMEONE BY once an hour," Sheriff Young said as Ruthann walked him through the studio to the door.

"Thank you, I do appreciate that. Oh! Do you want to take that pistol with you?"

He shook his head. "Keep it. Nate earned that one fair and square. Perhaps you should take it with you when you leave the studio. Have him show you how to use it, if you don't know."

Ruthann nodded. It was a good suggestion, even if she couldn't fathom carrying a gun in her pocket just to walk around the town where she'd spent her entire life.

Nor was she entirely sure Nate would show her how it worked, given the stricken look on his face when she'd pried the pistol from his fingers earlier.

"Thank you, Sheriff. Please give Penny my best," she said.

"She'll be around to visit again soon, I'm sure." Sheriff Young bid her farewell, and after he stepped out into the growing dusk, she secured the door behind him.

In the shadowy studio, she paused at the bottom of the stairs. Nate had been strangely quiet ever since he'd chased after that man. His eyes seemed far away, as if his mind had gone somewhere else entirely, and while he responded to the questions she and the sheriff had asked, his voice was flat.

What could she do to help him? Ruthann thought on that as she climbed the stairs. It was hard to know when she didn't understand specifically what bothered him so much to start with. He'd returned to Cañon City a different person than he was when he'd left, and it certainly had to do with the very little he'd told her about his time away. It was what caused that haunted sort of look in his eye she'd seen from time to time.

But that look had faded as the days went on—until now.

Whatever that man had said to him, it had brought Nate right back to where he'd been. And she couldn't help but wonder if it had something to do with the man's threat—the one Sissy had repeated to her in the general store.

Ruthann opened the door at the top of the stairs. Nate wasn't in the parlor, but a noise from the kitchen drew her attention. Closing the door, she made her way to the rear of their little apartment.

"Nate?" she asked when she entered the kitchen.

He stood over the table, a hunk of cheese sitting uncut before him. "I thought I'd find us something to eat."

Ruthann drew out a chair. "Why don't you sit, and I'll do that?"

Silently, he sank into the chair. Ruthann found a knife and began slicing the cheese. She retrieved the remainder of the bread she'd baked that morning, along with some butter and jam. "Tomorrow I'll make something warm and filling," she said as she slid a plate in front of Nate.

"This is fine." He picked up a slice of bread, but he didn't bite into it.

Ruthann sat, but any hunger she'd felt was gone too. She pushed her plate aside and gathered her hands into her lap. "May I ask what happened? When you went after that man?"

She held her breath as Nate set his bread down. When he looked up, he seemed to look right through her. Ruthann said nothing else; she waited patiently for Nate to speak.

"I brought him down and took that pistol from him. But then he got away."

It was more than that. The inkling Ruthann had earlier grew into something more certain.

She swallowed, twisting her hands together as she tried to figure out how to relay the threat to him. "When he grabbed hold of me by the gunsmith's, he mentioned something about the entire town finding out what sort of person you were." She spoke quietly, and Nate closed his eyes in response. "Is that what he said to you too?"

He nodded, his eyes going to his plate.

"I assumed it was something he'd made up to appear more threatening, or that it was foolish gossip Sissy had started and he'd heard." She trailed off, hoping he might agree.

But instead he pressed his lips together as he looked back up at her, and she could see in his eyes that the man had said the same to him.

And that he knew why.

Ruthann unclasped her hands. Gently, she reached out and laid one hand on Nate's. "Tell me."

"It's nothing."

Her heart ached for him. "Was it something that happened while you were in the cavalry? Was it losing Apollo?" She couldn't imagine how much losing his horse would have hurt him.

He shook his head. "It's nothing for you to worry over. What's done is done, and it isn't something fit to discuss." With that he pulled his hand away and stood.

Half alarmed at his brusqueness and half frustrated with his insistence upon keeping it to himself, Ruthann rose too. "I'd like to know. Please tell me about it."

He gave one decisive shake of his head. "It belongs in the past. I did nothing wrong—far from it, in fact—and that's all that matters."

"Of course you didn't. I know the man you are, Nate Harper, and you're nothing if not honorable and brave."

He winced, and Ruthann paused. What had she said to make him look as if she'd wounded him? She pressed her hands against her skirts and decided to come about it another way. "Sissy said something similar to me in the general store the other day. That's why I thought she might have been sharing some rumor she'd devised about you. Why do you suppose she would say something like that?"

"I don't know." Nate ran an impatient hand through his hair, hair that Ruthann normally would have longed to touch, but now she felt . . . distant. As if he'd put up a wall between the two of them, one designed to keep her out.

"I'm sorry," he said, sighing as he dropped his hand and saw the look on her face. "I imagine Sissy picked up on some gossip and was simply repeating it."

But where had she heard such a thing? The unanswered question hung between them.

"Perhaps he's a drifter, coming down from the mountains." Nate shrugged, but he still wouldn't meet Ruthann's eyes. "Can you set that aside for me?" He gestured at his plate. "I'd like to get some work done."

It was possible that the man was a drifter, Ruthann thought as the door closed behind Nate. And he'd simply picked up on some awful story being told among soldiers who'd known Nate.

But what *was* it?

Ruthann let air out through her teeth in frustration. He wouldn't tell her. And while she respected that he wished to leave the past where it was, how could she be of any help if she didn't know what had happened? Because clearly, it was something of terrible importance. Big enough to sit inside him and change his entire personality. Big enough for people like that man to use as a threat. Big enough for Sissy to throw at Ruthann.

Sissy . . . Ruthann stood and picked up the two plates filled with uneaten food. It was odd that she seemed to know about it too. Nate had brushed it off as a rumor, or overheard gossip, but what if it wasn't?

Ruthann nearly dropped the plates as the realization came to her, so obvious she wondered why she hadn't put it together before.

What if Sissy and the man who had chased Ruthann and Norah knew each other?

Chapter Twenty-two

THE CONVERSATION BETWEEN Nate and Ruthann had been strained in the two days since Nate had gone after the man who'd followed his wife and Norah. Nate wanted to pretend it hadn't been, but it was impossible to ignore the resentful look he caught in her eye from time to time. She didn't bring up his past again, and for that, at least, he was thankful. He could only hope she would forgive him and let it all go as more time passed.

Provided the man with the scar had disappeared for good.

They were spending a quiet evening, reading by lamplight, when a knock came from downstairs. Nate glanced at his pocket watch—the nice, new one Ruthann had given him for his birthday. It was after nine o'clock, far too late for visitors. Without a word, he picked up one of the lamps and headed downstairs, Ruthann following him.

Unlocking the door, he found Harry Caldwell, a gruff, older fellow who was one of Sheriff Young's regular deputies.

Before Nate could greet him, Caldwell spoke. "There's word of a gang of outlaws up north of town, supposedly lurking around. A few of them had a run-in with a lady out by the edge of town earlier. We're rounding up some men to head on up there, see if we can find them. Can we count on you?" He paused, and as if he'd just remembered his manners, tugged on the brim of his hat and nodded at Ruthann. "Ma'am."

"Good evening, Deputy," Ruthann said.

And as Caldwell asked after Ruthann's family, Nate's mind lurched into motion. He should go. He *ought* to go, as a member of this community, as a man with a family and a business to protect. And he knew why Caldwell had come here. As a former soldier, Nate was the ideal choice.

Six years ago, he would have jumped at the prospect to help round up outlaws threatening Cañon City. In fact, just three days ago, he would have gladly assisted without a second thought. But now . . .

Could he do it? Or would he freeze as he'd done the other day?

Caldwell's attention was back on him. He was a larger man, with a mustache and graying hair. In all his life, Deputy Caldwell would never understand why a younger man, a soldier, like Nate wouldn't agree to accompany him.

He had no choice, not if he wanted to keep his dignity intact—not only with the town, but with himself. He wouldn't let this town think he was a coward, not while he still held a breath in his body.

And so, against all of his better judgment, Nate nodded. "I'll go."

"Good. Meet us up by the livery in thirty minutes." And with that, the deputy was on his way.

Nate shut the door, and when he turned, Ruthann was watching him.

"Are you certain you want to go?" She asked the question in the most careful, loving manner possible. There was no hint of reproach or skepticism.

And instead of letting himself pretend that everything was fine, he let out a breath, closed his eyes for a second, and said, "I'm not, at all. But I have no choice."

Ruthann nodded. "I'd rather you not, but I understand."

Nate swallowed. He didn't deserve her. Never in a million years would someone like him deserve a woman like Ruthann. Yet here she was.

He led the way back upstairs. She waited in the kitchen while he changed and retrieved the guns he'd brought home from the Army. They felt foreign in his hands, and the bile rising in his throat when he touched them almost made him give this endeavor up altogether. Only the thought of the entire town laughing at him made him slide the pistols into their holsters.

He could only hope he wouldn't need them. He'd be fine otherwise. Or he could at least pretend as though he was.

When Nate entered the kitchen, Ruthann pressed a small wrapped bundle into his hands.

"Food. I don't know how long you'll be out there, and I don't want you to go hungry." She gave him an encouraging smile.

"Thank you." He added the food to the saddlebag he'd slung over his shoulder. "I ought to go."

Ruthann wrapped her arms around herself, and Nate wished she'd wrap them around him instead. But he'd put something between them, and he couldn't push through it, not now. And he feared he never would unless he told her more of what she wanted to know.

But how could he do that? It took everything he had right now to suppress it so he could get through the day. Bringing it out into the open . . . the prospect yawned like a never-ending fall off a cliff. It didn't deserve the light of day.

Besides, he didn't know if he could handle the way Ruthann might look at him afterward. What she might truly think of him.

Coward.

The word lurked around the edges of his mind. But he hadn't gone yellow. He knew that . . . didn't he?

It was more than he could think about right now. And so with one last look at Ruthann, standing alone with her arms wrapped around herself and her beautiful eyes glowing with a sadness he hoped he hadn't put there, he slipped out the door.

Chapter Twenty-three

WITH A SUDDEN START, Ruthann awoke.

She lay in bed, her eyes wide and her heart pounding faster than a train across the plains. What had woken her? Perhaps it had been a dream.

Letting out her breath, her heartbeat slowed as she turned over and resettled herself. It had been hard enough falling asleep knowing Nate was out there, somewhere, hunting down a gang of outlaws. Something she knew deep inside that he had no business doing at all, especially after what had happened with the man at the edge of town the other day.

Ruthann closed her eyes again and said another prayer for her husband. She only needed him to come back safely. Then they could talk more. What could she say that would convince him to let her hear the worries that seemed to consume him whole at times? He'd been so closed off when—

A crash sounded from downstairs.

Ruthann sat up in bed, her hands flat on either side of her. Her heart had seemed to stop altogether this time.

It could be Nate. Of course, that was the most logical answer. She didn't know what time it was, but perhaps their search had been fruitless and they'd returned quickly back to Cañon City.

But Nate knew his way around the studio better than anyone. Even in the dark.

Another crash sounded, this one accompanied by the sound of glass breaking.

It wasn't Nate.

Ruthann's stomach seemed to heave up somewhere in the vicinity of her heart. Whoever was downstairs was someone who shouldn't be there.

She ought to lock the apartment door. And then shove a piece of furniture against it, the settee perhaps. That's what Nate would want her to do. That's what would keep her the safest. Then whoever was making that noise downstairs could steal what they wished from the studio and be gone.

But what could they possibly want to steal? Nate didn't keep money down there. The only items of value were his photography equipment, and that was useless to anyone except a fellow photographer. There were two other photographers in town, and both had been perfectly friendly to Nate. In fact, they'd all met up for lunch a time or two to discuss the profession and the latest advances in it. If it was a thief downstairs, he was going to find himself sorely disappointed.

There was only one other possibility, and Ruthann felt sick just thinking about it.

She had a choice to make: lock and bar the door or confront the intruder.

Hands trembling, Ruthann wrapped a shawl around herself. It would take too long to put her shoes on. Besides, she'd be quieter barefoot. As another crash sounded from downstairs, she crossed the room to her trunk, where she'd stowed the gun Nate had taken from the blond man with the scar.

Originally, she'd put it in the parlor, but he'd kept looking at it as if its very presence bothered him, so she'd tucked it away in the bedroom.

Now, it felt cold and weighty in her hand—and she didn't have the first inkling about how to use it. But hopefully that wouldn't matter. All she needed to do was scare away whoever it was downstairs.

She crossed silently across the parlor to the door. She paused for a moment and pressed her ear to the wood. The sound of footsteps floated up, as did some words. Ruthann couldn't make out what they were saying, but it was clear there were two distinct voices. At least it wasn't more.

When the sound of something shattering made her jump, she placed her hand on the doorknob. It was now or never.

She turned the knob and prayed. Nate would want her to stay safe. But she couldn't, not when she knew someone was down there destroying everything he'd worked for. She would never forgive herself if she stayed up here and hid in the dark when she could have defended his business.

Letting out one deep, shuddering breath, she pressed the door open. With the gun held out in front of her in what she hoped was a convincing manner, Ruthann slowly stepped down the stairs.

Every noise was clearer out here. The items they tossed against the walls, the heavy fall of their boots, and—

"Oughtta take this," one of them said. "It's a shame to leave it."

"We ain't here for stealing," the other one replied just as the sound of something tumbling to the ground echoed across the room.

Ruthann swallowed, trying to suppress the very strong desire to turn around and run right back up the stairs. She pressed herself against the wall instead, as flat as possible.

"Suppose she's heard us?" The first man chuckled after he spoke, and Ruthann realized he was talking about *her*.

"Had to have by now. Come on, let's finish and get out of here. Maybe we'll finally get paid." The second man spoke brusquely, as if this were all about business for him.

Ruthann's insides twisted. They knew she was here. They'd come here on purpose, during a time when she was alone. For what? To scare her?

Instead of frightening her, the thought made her stiffen her shoulders and frown. Well, one thing was for certain. They didn't know she was right there. And they didn't know she was holding a gun.

Fire raged up from somewhere inside. These men were here to scare her and, she suspected since she couldn't see around the wall, destroy Nate's studio.

They didn't think she'd come downstairs, much less fight back. She only wished whoever it was that was paying them was here too.

Armed with the knowledge that her presence downstairs would surprise them—and the pistol in her hand—Ruthann stepped down the last two stairs and emerged into the studio.

It was dark, but her eyes had grown accustomed to it as she'd hidden on the stairs. It was hard to see the extent of the mess these men had made, but it was clear enough that furniture had been overturned and the place made to look ransacked.

And there, in the middle of the studio, stood two men. One held a piece of Nate's equipment that Ruthann couldn't put a name to, while the other was empty-handed. They both had the lower half of their faces covered, and neither had spoken in a raspy voice or had blond hair.

Neither one of these men was the one to whom the gun in her hands belonged.

She raised the weapon and waited for them to notice her. One finally did, dropping the equipment he held. Ruthann winced as it clattered against the floor.

He pushed the arm of his compatriot, who turned and stilled when he spotted Ruthann.

"I'll kindly ask you to leave my home," she said in a voice that sounded much braver than she felt.

The man who'd been empty-handed raised his hands now. "I thought you said she was upstairs."

"Didn't say nothing of the kind," the other man responded. "Look here, lady, we don't mean you no harm."

"Your actions say otherwise." Thank goodness it was dark, or they'd be able to see her hands shaking for certain. All she had to do was make them believe she would use this gun—and get them out. "It's past time for you to leave."

She should ask them questions. Find out why they were here. Why they felt the need to destroy Nate's hard work. If they knew the man who had cornered her outside in broad daylight.

Whether they knew Sissy.

But she didn't entirely trust her voice to remain strong. And the longer they stayed, the more likely it was that they'd notice she was utterly terrified.

"All right, we're going," the more reasonable of the two men said.

"We weren't done yet," the other replied.

"We're *done.*" He reached out and pushed the other man forward, toward the door.

Ruthann stepped back as the men passed. She willed her hands to steady and her eyes to remain steely as the more irritated of the two glared at her as he passed. His blue eyes were so bright there was no mistaking the color even in the gray shadows of night.

The first man opened the door and slipped outside. The second, the blue-eyed man, began to follow, but paused halfway through.

"Your husband had this coming. Give him our regards." And then he was gone.

Ruthann stood there for what felt like hours, afraid to move. Afraid to lower the gun. Afraid to get nearer to the door.

Slowly, the anger she'd used to propel herself to do something she never could have imagined yesterday began to subside. Her breath shuddered, and her arms ached as she lowered them. Before she lost her nerve, she stepped along the edge of the room to avoid broken glass and slid the bolt into the lock.

They must have forced their way in through the back door. Pushing aside her need to run upstairs and collapse into tears, Ruthann carefully made her way to the rear of the building. The glass in the back door was shattered. There wasn't much she could do about that right now, even if her mind had been perfectly clear. She locked the door and then dragged the stool—which, thankfully, wasn't broken—from Nate's darkroom to prop beneath the handle.

It wouldn't do much good, but fatigue had begun to work its way through her body. She'd lock and secure the door upstairs, just in case this didn't hold.

Back upstairs, she did just that. And then she huddled on the floor and cried as she never had in her life.

Chapter Twenty-four

IT WAS DARKER THAN sin and chillier than a summer night had any right to be up in the hills beyond town. They'd been out here for hours, traipsing up and down trails, scattering night creatures and startling an older man who lived alone in a moldering old cabin.

But there had been no sign of any outlaw gang.

As the hours passed, Nate began to relax. Even the sheriff and the other men seemed less on edge. If that gang was still nearby, they'd certainly moved farther away from town.

Sheriff Young rode up alongside Nate's horse. "It's getting close to dawn. They've likely moved on. We'll head home for now."

Nate nodded as relief flooded through him. The sheriff left to pass on the information to the other men, and Nate let his mind wander away from worry and toward a good few hours of sleep—and Ruthann.

Ruthann . . . If they were going to remain married, he needed to do something to remove the distance he'd created between them. Something that didn't involve him needing to tell her the details that lurked in his memories. *If* they were to remain married . . .

He smiled at the idea. It was absolutely what he wanted. And he imagined she felt the same way. Stuart would be angry.

As soon as he figured out how to repair things between himself and Ruthann—and ensured she wanted the same as he did—he'd need to surmise the best way to first, break the news to Stuart, and second, do that without losing his friendship.

You can't keep her safe.

He ground his teeth at the thought. It was one instance. Only one. He'd come to her aid more than once before that, after all.

"Harper!" The strained, urgent whisper broke through Nate's thoughts. It had come from Jasper Hill, the general store owner, who was bringing up the rear of the group immediately behind Nate.

Nate turned to find the man stopped on his horse and staring into a darkened copse of trees and brush. Heart lurching, Nate slowly walked his horse around.

Hill motioned at the trees as he drew a pistol. Nate's breath caught in his throat. He peered into the darkness.

Something moved.

Instinctively, his hand went to one of the revolvers at his hip even as his body recoiled at the thought of needing to pull it out. He glanced down the trail. A couple of men had noticed them stop and sat, waiting. The rest of the group was out of sight, somewhere farther down the trail.

Hill nudged his horse forward a couple of steps. Reluctantly, Nate did the same.

Whoever was behind the trees moved again. Didn't he see them out here? If he did, why didn't he remain still?

The movement intensified, and Hill raised his gun. The men off to the side had drawn their weapons too.

Only Nate hadn't. He *had* to. If he didn't, he'd be at a severe disadvantage if the outlaw emerged from his hiding place—or if he started shooting.

Do it, Nate told himself. *Now*. His fingers twitched, but the second they flexed over the grip, he froze.

Something inside wouldn't let him.

That was ridiculous. He had control of his own body. He reached again for the weapon, forcing himself to grab hold of it.

But that was as far as he got before the memories crowded in. *Screaming. Blood. Chaos.* He closed his eyes, willing them away, but they wouldn't go.

His eyes flew open as the leaves on the bushes and trees rustled again. Hill glanced at Nate, his brows drawn, before turning his attention back to the edge of the trail.

Nate forced himself to keep his eyes locked on what was before him, although the images of the past stubbornly played across his mind. His fingers sat frozen on the grip of his pistol, unmoving.

He was entirely unprepared for what was about to happen. This was even worse than when he'd run after the scarred man in town. At least then, he'd been able to grab the gun and aim it.

This time was much worse.

He was getting worse.

Nate shook his head, trying to clear that thought, but it stuck like glue against the images of the sobbing mother, the bleeding braves, the children . . . The children. All he wanted was to squeeze his eyes shut and force them back into the dark, but they wouldn't go and he couldn't close his eyes.

The memories were going to kill him.

The movement came again, closer this time, and shaking the entire large bush that sat near the trail. Next to him, Hill stiffened, his pistol aimed. The men off to the side stepped their horses closer.

And Nate sat, unmoving and stuck in the past as he watched the present play out before him.

There was a growl and a huff, and the branches of the bush snapped as someone emerged.

Not *someone*, but something.

A bear.

Next to him, one of the other men let out a string of curse words and raised his pistol.

"Don't shoot," Hill commanded. "If you miss, you'll anger it. Let's back away. See if it stays put."

Nate sat, stiff and unmoving on his horse, his fingers still curled around the pistol's grip. Hill shuffled backward on his horse, and behind him, Nate could hear the other men retreating too.

"Harper!" Hill's sharp tone finally pulled Nate from his statue-like state. "Let's go."

Feeling as if he hadn't moved in a month, Nate nodded slowly. He forced his hand back to the reins, flexing stiff fingers, and nudged the horse around.

The bear stayed where it was, its attention half on the men and half on the berries it had found growing in the bush.

"Easy does it," Hill said as they went.

Not until they were in the clear did Nate feel as if he could breathe again. The memories had subsided, but he still felt them, ghostly and menacing, threatening his very existence.

They'd nearly gotten him killed.

"You all right?" Hill asked as they rode along the trail that led back to town.

Nate nodded, not trusting himself with words.

Hill seemed to accept that, but the truth was, Nate wasn't all right. He was a broken, useless, *cowardly* mess.

What would have happened if Ruthann had been with him? What if they had children? What if that *hadn't* been a bear, and instead was an outlaw with nothing to lose? Nate's inability to act had put everyone in danger, not just himself.

As the first light of day appeared on the horizon and they crested the last hill above town, Nate knew for certain what he'd feared all along.

He couldn't be a husband. He certainly couldn't be a father. He couldn't protect himself, much less anyone else.

Much less a family.

From the start, he'd told himself that no matter his feelings, Ruthann deserved someone better than him. Someone who didn't fight every day to keep memories from consuming him.

And definitely not a man who couldn't even pull a gun. Not a man who could hardly focus on the moment because the past was too present in his mind.

Perhaps he was the coward that man had said he was, no matter what Nate had told himself.

A deep, lonely sadness enveloped him as he determined what he needed to do next. He'd do what he'd promised from the start, and he'd set Ruthann free. She might be broken-hearted, but at least she'd be safe. And if it hadn't been long enough to repair his reputation from Miss Flagler's campaign for marriage, then so be it. Her life was far more important than his business or his standing in town.

When he returned home, he'd insist upon an annulment.

Chapter Twenty-five

RUTHANN COULDN'T SLEEP. She'd dozed for perhaps an hour, and then found herself headed downstairs with a broom and a bucket the second it was light enough to see without a lamp.

She paused at the bottom of the stairs. Her heart pinched at the sight before her. Nate's studio looked as if a train had run through it. Broken glass and porcelain lay scattered across the floor. Furniture was overturned, and they'd even taken a knife to the settee and torn the cushion. Something stained the wall, and it took her a moment to determine it was coffee, likely from the cup Nate had taken downstairs with him the day before and had forgotten about.

Drawing up every ounce of bravery she had and praying with all her heart, Ruthann crossed toward his darkroom where she'd taken the stool from last night. Opening the door to let the light in, she glanced around the room.

By all miracles, it was intact. They must have started their path of destruction from the front of the studio. It made sense, considering they would have wanted to ensure the place was empty—and that she was upstairs.

Grateful that most of Nate's precious photography equipment was safe, Ruthann began attacking the mess on the floor. She hadn't gotten very far when the front door opened and

Nate's figure appeared in the first rays of morning sun shining in from outside.

She immediately set aside her broom and dustpan and went to meet him. He'd paused just inside the door, where he ran a hand over his tired face and then peered again across the studio.

Ruthann came to his side. She went to reach for him, paused, and then forced herself to cast aside her doubts and wrapped an arm around his waist. He went stiff under her touch, and her heart ached. She wanted so badly to comfort him. Instead, she pulled her arm away, but remained close. Seeing what was before him must be a great shock, and she refused to let him face it alone.

"They came last night," she said. "Two men, neither of whom I recognized."

He looked at her then, fire blazing in his eyes. "They came upstairs? Did they hurt you?"

"No, not at all. The noise they made woke me up, and so I took that pistol the sheriff said to keep and came down here."

His eyes widened. "Why would you do that?"

She put her hands on her hips. "I wasn't about to let them destroy all of your work. I was able to run them off. They were just about gone when . . ." She bit her lip, debating whether it mattered if Nate knew what that man had said.

"What?" he demanded.

It was best he knew everything, she supposed. "One of them said that you 'had it coming.'"

Nate shook his head as he surveyed the room again. "This is . . . it's too much." He sighed in a way that made her feel as if he were ready to give up.

On one hand, she could hardly blame him. How could he fight something—or someone—when he didn't know why this was happening? Would Sissy go this far in her revenge? She might still harbor anger toward him, but Ruthann doubted she would do anything to jeopardize her courtship with her new beau.

On the other hand . . . Ruthann refused to let Nate give up everything he'd worked so hard for.

"This is easily cleaned up," she said, determining to give him as much strength as she could to ensure he kept going, kept trying, kept fighting. "It won't take but an hour or two. They didn't touch the equipment in the darkroom. You can be back to work today, provided nothing essential is broken. We can lay a quilt over the settee." She gestured at where the cushion had been torn.

He shook his head as if it were all hopeless. "It's all I have."

Ruthann's breath caught in her throat. "It isn't," she whispered. "I'm here."

"I can't . . ." When he looked at her, Ruthann thought she might shrivel under the war of emotions playing out in his eyes.

He looked away again, staring off at the wall. "It's time I see about getting that annulment."

Every heartbeat felt like an eternity as Ruthann tried to make sense of his words. "Why?" was all she could seem to say.

"It's what I promised, isn't it? To you and to your brother. It's past time I followed through."

"No." Fire shot up from somewhere deep inside her. She would not give up that easily. "Nate."

At her insistence, he looked at her again, but instead of seeing sadness, anger, *anything*, all she saw was an emptiness. As if he'd pushed every emotion away and was left with nothing.

And in that moment, she wanted something from him. Anything that would show she meant as much to him as he did to her.

"All of this time we've shared, all of these moments, do they mean nothing to you?"

His jaw worked, but he didn't answer. Instead he looked somewhere over her shoulder, as if he'd already left the room—and left her.

"I think . . ." She summoned the thoughts that had come into her mind more than once, ever since he'd first gone cold toward her, when his past had seemed to cloud out his future. "I think that you believe *you* aren't enough. For yourself, for me, for anyone. But you are, Nate. You are more than enough. You're kind and thoughtful and funny and sweet and brave."

His jaw clenched again and he shook his head. "You don't understand. You weren't there. No one can understand."

She wasn't where? At first she thought he meant up in the hills, or perhaps when he'd gone after that man who had followed her and Norah. But that look . . . His eyes had gone from empty to tortured again, just as they had when he'd been reminded of the past.

He meant in the Dakota Territory. In the cavalry.

"You're right, I can't truly understand. But I can listen. I can help you."

"There is no help." He looked at her then, those brown eyes catching hers. Even now—even when she felt as if she was losing him—they still took her breath away. "You don't deserve someone like me."

His words were like an arrow through her heart. He thought so little of himself that it physically hurt Ruthann to see it. "I do. No one is made perfectly, Nate. We all have flaws."

"This is more than a *flaw*. It's a defect of character." He rubbed an impatient hand over his chin. "I'm useless, and you need someone who can keep you safe."

"No." Ruthann shook her head defiantly. "What if I refuse?"

"This is what you agreed to, remember?" His words had an edge to them. He wanted her to think he was angry with her, that he didn't care.

Ruthann didn't believe it for a minute.

"I don't care what I agreed to. I've changed my mind." She crossed her arms and fixed him with the most determined look she could muster.

Nate let out an irritated sigh. "Ruthann—"

"*No*. We are married, for better and for worse."

"It was a farce." His voice had grown angrier, but Ruthann stood her ground, her arms held against her chest and her chin raised. She would fight for this marriage even if he wanted to give up.

And then he did something she'd never seen him do—he raised a fist and slammed it into the nearby wall.

Ruthann gave a squeak, a hand flying to her mouth.

He flexed his hand and she instinctively took a step forward, reaching out to see what damage he'd caused himself. But he pulled his hand away as if she were made of fire.

"You aren't listening to me," he said in a voice made of steel. "I said this is over. All of it. There is nothing here, nothing between you and me but a temporary agreement. I thank you for your help, and I'll find a lawyer in the morning."

With that, he turned and walked toward the door.

"Nate!" Ruthann began to walk after him.

"Ruthann Joliet," he said, turning around, his teeth gritted. "Don't follow me. I don't want you to. I don't . . . I don't want *you*."

He might as well have punched her in the stomach instead of that wall. Ruthann pressed her hands against her abdomen as he stalked out, the door slamming behind him.

She'd thought he was giving up, but this was more than that.

He didn't want *her*.

He didn't care for her. After everything—their quiet conversations, the sweet gestures he'd shown her, the kisses—he'd decided he didn't want her.

I shouldn't believe it. But his words were too harsh, the look on his face too cold.

It didn't matter whether she believed him or not. He'd decided he was done. And there wasn't a thing she could do about it.

And with that thought, she crumpled to the floor for the second time that day as tears welled up in her eyes and began to spill.

Chapter Twenty-six

NATE DIDN'T RETURN until after dark. To his relief, Ruthann wasn't there. And neither were many of her things. The apartment above the studio was too empty and too quiet without her presence. Nate gave it one hour, until it seemed that both guilt and the ghosts in his mind would consume him whole if he stayed here by himself.

He spent the night at the boardinghouse and didn't venture back to the studio until late in the morning. It seemed word had gotten around about how his studio had been ransacked, because he arrived to find no customers waiting.

It was easier to avoid thinking about Ruthann when he kept busy, so Nate set to work cleaning up the mess in the studio. His hand was black and blue from his outburst yesterday, but the pain seemed almost a penance for what he'd done. For how he'd hurt Ruthann.

As he reached the rear of the studio, he knew he'd have to order new glass for the window in the back door, but in the meantime, he covered it with a burlap sack, cut open to cover the hole. If Ruthann were here, he had no doubt she would have sewn up something prettier to cover the broken window.

That thought made his heart ache, and so he pushed it away and picked up the broom again.

A few minutes later, the front door opened. Nate tensed, sure it was one of the men who had turned his studio upside down. But it was only Stuart, who paused once inside and frowned at the partially swept-up room.

"Ruthann told me what had happened, but it was hard to believe until I saw it myself." He closed the door behind him and went right to the little end table, which still lay on its side, and set it upright. He dusted his hands together. "I'd say someone has it out for you."

Nate leaned the broom against the wall. Ruthann had occupied so much of his mind that he hadn't had the wherewithal to think about that. But it was true. Someone certainly was out to ruin him, and their actions were growing more daring by the day. "It appears that way," he finally said.

"Have you any thoughts about who it might be? Because I certainly do."

Nate rubbed his forehead with his unbruised hand. "Sissy Flagler." He went on to tell Stuart about how the scarred man's words echoed those Miss Flagler had spoken to Ruthann in Hill's General Store. Of course, how either of them knew about his experience in the Army was a looming, unanswered question.

Stuart nodded thoughtfully. "It has to be her. Her father's money could buy any number of men desperate enough to chase a lady down in the street or break into a business in the dead of night. The only question is how to prove it."

Nate didn't have a solution for that conundrum. He wondered if Ruthann would. The very thought of her—her sweet smile, those lovely blue eyes, her simple joy in seeing him happy—made his stomach clench with regret. He closed his eyes at the pain. *It was for the best.*

"Are you all right?"

Stuart's question made Nate's eyes fly open. It was almost as if he'd forgotten his friend was present.

"I'm fine," he said shortly as he reached for the broom.

"Really?" Stuart arched an eyebrow. "Because it doesn't seem so." He paused. "Ruthann isn't doing so well either."

Nate's fingers clamped harder around the broom handle at that news. What did he think? That Ruthann would return home to her parents, forget all about him, and go on with her life? While that would have made him feel better about his decision, he knew better. That vision of her heartbreak spilling out all around them as he told her he didn't want her was all too vivid in his mind. He clenched his jaw at the thought of her feeling such sorrow over him. It certainly wasn't something she deserved, and he'd been the one who'd caused it.

But it was for the best . . . wasn't it?

"I'm sorry to hear that," he said carefully, keeping his words measured just so in order to avoid conveying the emotion that welled up inside like a torrent of rain against a dam.

"To be honest, I'm surprised," Stuart replied.

That got Nate's attention. He looked up from where he'd begun sweeping. "It was what we'd agreed to. I thought you'd be happy about it."

"Well . . ." Stuart nodded slowly, as if he were considering Nate's words. He ran a hand over his jacket and then dropped it to his side. "I might've been wrong."

Nate didn't know what to say to that. At least, nothing that wouldn't make him feel even worse about sending Ruthann away.

"Look, I thought I was protecting my sister. It was obvious she had feelings for you when we were younger, and when you left . . . Well, she would never admit it to me, but I could see how unhappy she was. But I've never seen her so happy, as she's been since marrying you." He paused. "And in the past few weeks, you've seemed happier too. Which is why I don't understand what's happened."

Nate began sweeping again, as if the act of moving around the debris on the floor would push away the remorse threatening to undo him. "It wouldn't work. It's better this way."

"That's not good enough," Stuart said.

"It isn't your concern."

Stuart clasped his hand around the broom handle, stilling it. "It is. My sister is despondent with grief and my oldest friend is denying himself the one thing that would make him happiest."

Nate didn't reply, but he let go of the broom. Stuart didn't know the images that tortured him. And he didn't know how those memories affected Nate in a way that endangered Ruthann.

"Does this have something to do with what happened the other night? When you were out searching for those outlaws? Ruthann said that when you returned, you were different."

Nate clenched his jaw.

"For the love of Jupiter, Nate. Spit it out. You've been keeping enough secrets since you've come back. If you can't tell my sister, then tell me."

Nate ran his hands over his face. He had to say something. Goodness knew, Stuart wouldn't leave him alone otherwise. "I can't protect her, all right? I couldn't even protect myself up there. You weren't there. You didn't see me freeze up. Jasper Hill probably thinks I've lost my mind, the way I sat there on the horse. I couldn't draw, I couldn't do anything." He drew in a breath, steadying his ragged voice. "Ruthann deserves better."

Stuart nodded slowly, but he didn't speak. It was almost as if he were waiting for Nate to say more.

But when Nate didn't, Stuart shoved his hands into his pockets. "All right. I hear you. I'll speak with her."

That was it. Stuart left, and Nate stood there, wondering what his friend meant. Speak to Ruthann about what? About what a coward her husband was? About how smart it would be to let Nate move forward with the annulment?

He should have been happy with how the conversation ended, but instead he just felt empty inside.

Stuart agreed with him, clearly. He was a coward, and nothing could change that.

But even as he told himself that and took up the broom again, memories of Ruthann came unbidden into his mind. Her kisses, her kind words, the little gestures that let him know she cared for him.

They filled up the empty place inside. He'd let that all go. Given it all away.

It was for the best.

Even if he loved her.

Chapter Twenty-seven

"IF YOU STARE AT THAT wall much longer, you'll bore a hole into it." Stuart's voice came from somewhere behind Ruthann.

She turned, and there he was, lurking in her bedroom doorway. Ruthann stood and sighed. It was dreary outside, and the weather matched her mood. Just a few days ago, she'd felt as if she had so much to look forward to, and now . . . nothing. Not a single thing gave her joy. Talking with Norah, seeing the new hats that had come in from back East at Mrs. Claver's, visiting with Mrs. Sample and her new baby that morning, the glow of the sunset last night—all of it had left her feeling exhausted and dull. It unnerved her family, she could tell. Even her own mother had avoided discussing the reason for her return.

"What do you want?" she asked Stuart as she crossed the room.

He leaned against the doorframe, his hat in his hand. "I've just returned from visiting your husband."

"Oh?" She hated the way her curiosity was piqued at this revelation. Although Stuart had likely gone to thank Nate for finally ending their marriage, and that was not a conversation Ruthann cared to have recounted to her.

"Yes." He tapped his hat against his thigh and looked down.

Ruthann tilted her head. This wasn't the stance of a happy man. "Stuart? Why do you look so sheepish?"

He raised his eyes back up to her, and sheepish was absolutely the best choice of words to describe him. "I was wrong. You know it pains me to admit that. And so I went to Nate and told him so."

Ruthann didn't know what to say to that.

"Something is bothering him deeply, although I assume you already know that."

She nodded. "He would never tell me, no matter how much I pressed. It happened while he was in the Army, but that's all I know."

Stuart tossed his hat into a chair and crossed his arms. "He fears he can't keep you safe. He froze out there, the other night when he went up into the hills, when the time came for him to act. He thinks you deserve better."

Ruthann closed her eyes, her heart breaking all over again for him. "It's because of what happened in his past."

She opened her eyes and saw the same empathy she felt for Nate reflected in Stuart's eyes. It didn't matter what Nate had said to her. She'd been right when she thought she shouldn't believe it. He was doing what he thought was noble, what he thought was best for her—even if it tore them both apart.

"I love him," she whispered.

"I know," Stuart replied. "I believe he feels the same about you."

A lump grew in Ruthann's throat, and she turned, fighting back the tears that stung her eyes. Thankfully, Stuart said nothing as she fought to regain control of herself. The urge to cry finally subsided, and with it came a fierce desire to *do* something.

Nate might be bent, but he was not broken. He was much too strong for that, even if he didn't believe it himself.

"We have to help him," she said, clasping her hands together.

Stuart smiled. "I agree."

"And we ought to start with Sissy Flagler."

"She's the most likely suspect. If we can eliminate the immediate threats against him, perhaps things will begin to right themselves."

Ruthann nodded. It would take more than making Sissy cease her campaign against him, but it was a start. Nate would never feel at ease if Sissy kept opening his old wounds.

"Let me get ready, and we'll go immediately to pay Sissy a visit." Ruthann moved to her wardrobe.

"I'll meet you downstairs." Stuart grabbed his hat and left.

Ruthann removed a shawl, and then, perusing her small collection of hats, she chose the one she'd been wearing the day she'd met Nate, when he'd walked with her to help Mr. McGregor get home safely. Perhaps it would bring her luck again today.

She went to the mirror over her dressing table and sat to tie her hat. She would do the very best she could to get Sissy to confess and then extract a promise to call off the men she'd paid to make Nate's life miserable.

And then, Ruthann would fight for Nate himself. He deserved it, even if he didn't think he did. She would tell him how much she loved him. She would be there for him.

Hopefully that would be enough. But even if it wasn't, she would never give up—not on herself, and never on him.

Chapter Twenty-eight

THE STUDIO WAS BACK in order by late afternoon, just in time for a couple to come inquiring about a photograph. The man walked holding on to the arm of the woman Nate presumed was his wife. They were older than Nate, closer to his mother's age, if she'd still been living.

"Good afternoon," the man said when Nate greeted them. "We were hoping to have our photo taken. My wife and I are newly wed."

"Congratulations," Nate replied. "And certainly. You've come to the right place." He gestured to the settee. "I have chairs too, if that would be more comfortable."

"Oh, no, this is fine," the woman said. As they walked arm in arm, Nate noticed the man had a distinct limp. When he turned to sit, he grimaced some, but only for a moment before giving his wife a radiant smile.

"My Ellie is a blessing to me," he said. "She gives this old soldier life again."

"You were in the Army?" Nate paused at his camera.

"The War Between the States," the man said as his wife arranged herself next to him on the settee. "Bullet hit my knee, and I've never been the same since. I was lucky to keep my leg." His features drew in, as if he was remembering the exact moment. "What a loss of life. It's a miracle I escaped with only a lame leg."

Nate swallowed. The man's words hit far too close to home. He gripped the camera, trying to focus on what needed doing rather than falling headfirst into his customer's story and drowning. "Let me get some plates. Please, make yourselves comfortable."

He strode to the darkroom, closing the door behind him and taking deep breaths. This was not the only time he was going to run into a fellow soldier; in fact, it was already the second. He needed to remain calm and businesslike. But as he stood there, he realized it wasn't the old memories that were trying to push their way into his mind.

It was Ruthann.

Nate gripped the plates he'd picked up. She'd come to mind because of the couple in his studio. Because of the gentle way the woman had helped her husband, because of the love that shone in both their eyes . . . because of the acceptance she'd shown of his old wound.

All Nate could see was the man's injured leg, but based on what he'd said, he wondered if there wasn't more the man had struggled with. Or that he continued to struggle with.

And yet, he was—by all appearances—happily married.

Suddenly wanting to spend more time with the couple, he emerged from the darkroom. As he prepared the camera and instructed the two on how to sit and where to look, he asked questions. As it turned out, he didn't need to ask many. Both the man and his wife were happy to tell him about how they'd fallen in love. How she'd been widowed and he'd gone for years and years unable to find what he was looking for.

"Because," he said to Nate with a knowing smile, "I was looking to forgive myself. I just didn't know it until I met Ellie."

If Nate hadn't been holding on to the camera, the man's words would have sent him falling backward in surprise.

"Ellie saved my life." The old soldier reached over and squeezed his wife's hand.

"I do love you, too, Micah, but if we don't let this young man get on with his work, we'll be keeping him all night." The woman smiled kindly at her husband.

Nate went through the motions of taking their photograph. While they sat as still as possible and he waited for the exposure, he ran the man's words through his head again.

I was looking to forgive myself.

Was that what Nate needed too?

Yes.

The answer came like a gunshot through his mind, tearing through the specters of the past, through all his doubts and fears, through his inability to tell Ruthann what he'd experienced.

It made no sense whatsoever. How would forgiving himself help him keep Ruthann safe? Even if he did, it was no guarantee he could pick up a pistol without falling apart.

But as he watched the couple, he wondered. Was it forgiveness that made the man whole again?

There was no way to be sure, but as he finished the session and thanked the couple, he knew he wanted it.

He wanted everything they had for himself—peace, forgiveness, love. The question was whether he was brave enough to pursue it. And there was no way to find out unless he took the first step.

He would not be a coward about this.

Nate tucked away the plates with the couple's image in his darkroom. He would develop them in the morning. Right now, he needed to see Ruthann.

He'd just grabbed his hat and buttoned his jacket when the studio door opened. But it wasn't a customer this time.

It was Sissy Flagler.

Chapter Twenty-nine

TO RUTHANN'S DISMAY, Sissy had gone out for the evening. The Flaglers' housekeeper informed them that she'd left in a hurry not ten minutes ago.

Ruthann walked slowly down the Flaglers' front steps, Stuart at her side. "I suppose it will have to wait until tomorrow." She couldn't help her despondent tone. She'd wanted so much to finally get the truth from Sissy, and to, perhaps, put an end to the threats against Nate.

"We'll return in the morning," Stuart replied. He extended an arm, and Ruthann took it, grateful for his presence. It was nice to have someone as concerned as she was about Nate.

"I didn't thank you for your change of heart," she said, looking up at her older brother. "It means a lot to me."

He smiled and patted her hand. "I won't pretend it didn't pain me at first. But I'm not one to stand in the way of love. Although I still don't see why you couldn't find it with Foster Jones or Roscoe Waller."

Ruthann shook her head, smiling herself. Her brother would always be a brother, that much was for certain. "Weren't you the one who warned me about Mr. Waller's tooth grinding? I seem to recall you didn't much like either man when they courted me."

Stuart began to laugh, just as Sheriff Young approached them.

"Evening, Ben," Stuart said, trying to regain his composure. "I trust everything is peaceful in Cañon City tonight?"

"Even more so now that I've got one of the men who broke into Harper's Photographic Studio in my jail." The sheriff doffed his hat to Ruthann. "Good evening, Mrs. Harper. I was on my way to the studio to fetch you. I don't suppose you'd come identify the fellow?"

"Of course. I'd be happy to." Hope blazed in her heart. If they found one of the men, surely the others wouldn't be too far behind. And then Sissy would end her brigade to destroy Nate's livelihood and reputation.

"Caldwell caught him trying to make off with a crate of food from the general store. It didn't take much for him to confess he was also one of the men who broke into the studio. It seems he's not too happy about going unpaid for that deed, which is what made him resort to stealing food. He'll say more, I'm sure of it. He's that angry. But I want your corroboration first."

It wasn't far to the sheriff's office, and once there, Ruthann and Stuart followed Sheriff Young inside. The scent of dinner drifted down from the upstairs apartment where the sheriff lived with Penny, and Ruthann's stomach rumbled. She ignored it, however, the moment she laid eyes on the man in the jail cell in the back.

The sheriff had opened the door to where the cells were located in the rear of the building to let Ruthann and Stuart enter. The man with the bright blue eyes fairly glared at her from where he stood inside.

"Yes, that's him," she said to Sheriff Young. "They had the lower half of their faces covered, but I recognize his eyes."

"You're the reason I'm here. You and your husband," the man said to her.

"The reason you're here is because you snuck in the back of the general store without anyone noticing and tried to make off with enough food for six men," Sheriff Young replied.

It was a bold action, but so was entering the studio when he and his partner knew she was there. As the thought went through her mind, Ruthann furrowed her brow. They'd known she was there . . . and had known Nate wasn't. They'd only referred to her being upstairs while she'd hidden herself in the stairway.

"They knew Nate wasn't there that night," she said aloud. "How did you know that?" She directed her question to the man in the cell.

The man simply crossed his arms and continued to glare at her.

"The more helpful you are now, Peters, the better the word I can put in for you later," Sheriff Young said from the doorway.

"How good a word?" Peters didn't uncross his arms, but he suddenly looked less menacing.

"Depends on how useful your information is. I thought you were mad at being unpaid. Doesn't seem right that you're in here and the fellows who owe you aren't."

Ruthann looked back at the man in the cell. He slowly uncrossed his arms, and she held her breath. If he named Sissy, this would be easier than she'd thought.

Although how would Sissy know about the sheriff searching for outlaws in the hills outside of town?

"It was made up," Peters said. "The outlaw gang."

Ruthann glanced at the sheriff, who looked just as surprised as she felt.

"What do you mean?" Sheriff Young asked.

Peters' mouth curved up a little, as if this all amused him. "This other fellow mentioned to one of your deputies that there was trouble with a lady near the edge of town, and happened to think it was caused by a gang wanted out of Denver."

"But it was fabricated," Stuart said from behind Ruthann. "To get the sheriff out of town."

"And Nate," Ruthann added. She looked the man right in his eyes. "You knew they'd ask Nate to come along because of his background in the cavalry."

Peters shrugged but he didn't deny it.

"You purposefully endangered my sister?" Stuart was beside Ruthann now, his voice lowered.

She laid a hand on his arm. Getting angry at the man would do them no good. "You wanted to scare me. That much I heard you say the evening you and the other man were in the studio."

"That's about the gist of it." Peters flicked a glance at Stuart. "The lady wasn't ever in any danger. We ain't like that. Not me or the Sergeant. All we wanted was to get paid, not hanged."

"The Sergeant?" Sheriff Young asked.

"The one who was with me that night. Don't know his real name, and that's probably for the best. All I know is he was in the cavalry some time back so everyone calls him Sergeant. He's the one who got me and this other fellow called Jonesy—don't know where he's got off to since he got into it with Harper in the street—involved. Said it was good money." He paused. "Ain't seen any of that money yet, though."

Ruthann exchanged a glance with Stuart. If this Sergeant had been in the cavalry, he might have known Nate . . . and what had happened to him.

"Was it this Sergeant who orchestrated the break-in at the studio?" Sheriff Young asked.

Peters paused. He looked off to the side as if he were weighing what to tell them.

"You could move on over to the Territorial Prison tonight, if you'd be more comfortable there," Young said with a steely edge to his voice. "I'll walk you right on over there myself. While whoever it is that didn't pay you gets to run free."

Peters worked his jaw. "It wasn't the Sergeant. He got taken in, same as me and Jonesy."

Ruthann chewed her lip, waiting for him to speak Sissy's name. When he finally looked back toward her and Stuart, all she could think about was how quickly this could end for Nate. The sheriff could arrest the other men involved, and while Ruthann didn't know what would happen with Sissy, Nate would finally be free to build his business without looking over his shoulder.

They could talk. Perhaps she could even convince him to trust her with whatever darkness it was he carried with him. Whatever it was that this Sergeant seemed to know about. Perhaps—

"Right. He's a finely dressed fellow, younger than he looks, but don't really have money. He puts on airs, all because of this lady he's courting. She's the one with the money. He keeps saying he'll get it from her, but to be honest, I doubt she's going to give it to him. Especially when she finds out what he's been doing. He's the one that sought out the Sergeant."

Ruthann blinked at him. It wasn't Sissy at all.

"It's her new beau," she said.

"Do you know his name?" the sheriff asked her and Stuart.

"Paul," Ruthann said, pulling the name from when she'd run into Sissy at the general store. "That's what she called him."

"I'm going to the Flaglers," Sheriff Young said. "I can't leave Peters here alone and I need Caldwell with me. Stuart, would you—"

"Happy to," he replied.

But Ruthann's mind was on Nate. He needed to know. He deserved to know.

"I'm going to Nate," she announced as she was halfway out the door.

Chapter Thirty

SISSY FLAGLER DID NOT look well.

That was all Nate could think when she burst through the studio door, her eyes wild and her hair falling down from under her hat. She shut the door behind her and pressed a hand to her chest as she caught her breath. It appeared as if she'd been chased here.

"Miss Flagler? Did you—" Nate moved to the door and looked out the window. Nothing looked out of place on the street outside. He took a few steps back again. "Did you run here?"

She nodded, drawing in great gulps of air.

As much as Nate didn't want her here—or anywhere near him again—it was clear something was amiss, and he wasn't about to toss her onto the street without hearing it.

"Mr. Harper," she said finally, her voice still breathy. "I owe you an apology, but there isn't time for that right now. Please . . . does that door lock?" She nodded at the studio door.

Nate raised his eyebrows. "It does." He said the words carefully, the memory of how she acted the first time she was here all too fresh in his mind. "I can't say I'm comfortable with—"

She shook her head so vigorously that another lock of dark hair escaped its pin and tumbled down her back. "Please, it isn't that. You must lock the door, for your safety."

175

Nate looked at her curiously, but moved back to the door to do as she suggested. He reached for the bolt, but before he could grab hold of it the door burst open again. A familiar-looking man who lacked a significant amount of hair atop his head stood in the doorway. But it wasn't anything about the way he looked that gave Nate alarm—it was the pistol in his hand.

"Paul, please. You don't need to do this," Miss Flagler said.

Nate looked between her and the man with the gun, who had already shut the door behind him, and he realized where he'd seen the man before.

He was Miss Flagler's new beau. The one who had been with her at the church dance Nate had attended with Ruthann.

"On the contrary, Sissy, I do. I won't let any man make my intended look anything less than virtuous." His dark eyes glinted with malice as he looked at Nate. Then they narrowed before he turned his attention to Miss Flagler again. "Why are you here?"

Miss Flagler straightened her shoulders and lifted her chin before saying, "I overheard you speaking with the Sergeant."

The man called Paul shook his head. "You ought to be happy I'm doing this for you."

"I'm not, though. Don't you see?" She sounded as if she were on the verge of tears. "I don't care about him." She flung out a hand to indicate that she was speaking of Nate.

"But I do," the man said, his attention returning to Nate. He raised the pistol just slightly, and Nate lifted his hands, keeping them outstretched in front of him.

He had nothing with which to defend himself, although given his recent inability to do just that, it probably didn't matter. In fact, without a gun in his own hand, he could think. And he could speak. If he kept the man talking, then perhaps he could think of a way out of this situation.

"I'm sorry, I don't believe we've met," he said. "I'm Nate Harper."

"I know who you are," the man growled.

"His name is Paul Griffiths," Miss Flagler supplied, almost as if she were irritated that her beau had forgone social niceties.

"May I ask, Griffiths, why you're standing in my place of business with a pistol pointed at me?" If Nate were a gambling man, he would have laid down a tidy sum that the reason was Miss Flagler and her spurious accusation. But he wanted the man talking, and not shooting.

"You embarrassed my fiancée," Griffiths said.

"Fiancée?" Nate raised his eyebrows and glanced at Miss Flagler.

"It's . . . it's unannounced," she said, stumbling over the words.

Nate had all sorts of opinions about that on the tip of his tongue, but he kept those to himself, choosing only to say, "Congratulations. When do you plan to be married?"

"It's no business of yours," Griffiths replied sharply. "But I can't have any man going around and telling folks that Sissy is anything less than the good woman she is."

Nate also had many opinions on *that* statement. Although considering Miss Flagler attempted to warn him about Griffiths, he was on the verge of changing his general opinion about her. "I assure you, I've said nothing whatsoever about Miss Flagler."

Griffiths narrowed his eyes. "You lie."

"I do not." He had to tread carefully. If he insulted Miss Flagler at all, it might send this man over the edge—and Miss Flagler herself might regret her attempt to help him and join her fiancé instead. "There was a simple misunderstanding that is all over now. I'm happily married, and it appears you two will be also."

"A simple misunderstanding?" Griffiths shook his pistol. "Is that what you call—"

"*Paul*! Please, stop." Miss Flagler stepped forward now and wrapped her hands around his arm as she looked up at him. "Mr. Harper is being truthful."

Griffiths glanced at her quickly before returning his glare to Nate. "That isn't what you told me after we met. He led you on, and when your father pressed him for your hand, he tried to ruin your reputation by producing a fiancée from essentially nowhere, indicating that you had made it all up."

Tears rolled down Miss Flagler's face now. She looked at Nate, who returned her gaze with sympathy. As much as he'd come to dislike her for what she'd done, it was hard to feel anything but pity for the woman now.

"I did. I fabricated the story," she said softly through her tears. "I'm the one who pushed myself onto him, and when he acted the gentleman and refused me, I was angry."

Nate held his breath. Surely the man would realize she was speaking the truth and lower that gun.

But instead, he grunted and shook his head. "No. That isn't what you told me. And considering everything I've done hasn't driven Harper from town yet, I'll take care of him myself."

Keep him talking, Nate ordered himself, even as the man's expression grew harder and more dangerous.

"You were the one who sent men over here to tear up my studio and scare my wife," he said.

"You didn't," Miss Flagler whispered.

"It's the least he deserves," Griffith said, his eyes on Nate. "I want you gone from this town."

"And you sent that man after Ruthann—twice," Nate pressed as his mind searched for a way out of this situation.

"Only once, but Jonesy likes to do a thorough job. Or he did, anyhow. I don't know where he's gotten off to."

Miss Flagler was shaking her head, red-rimmed eyes looking at Griffiths like she didn't know a thing about any of this. "I thought those were only threats."

"I follow through on everything I say. I'm a man of my word," Griffiths replied. Then he frowned. "Unlike the Sergeant or the men he found."

Nate had been so preoccupied with the gun pointed at him the first time Griffiths had mentioned this Sergeant that he'd barely taken notice of it. But now . . .

"Were you in the Army?" he asked.

Griffiths gave a dry laugh. "Not me. I don't take orders well. But I'll say it wasn't difficult to track down that cavalry regiment you served with up in the Black Hills. And it was even easier to persuade one of those men to come down here and work for me. I don't know what you did to Robert Wallingford, but he jumped on the first train out of Denver at my telegram."

Nate fought to keep the surprise from his face. Wallingford had served with him at least half the time Nate had been in the cavalry. He hadn't done a thing to Wallingford, but . . . He closed his eyes. The man was a gambler. The lure of easy money was likely enough to turn him against a fellow soldier.

"He was never a sergeant," Nate said to keep the conversation going.

Griffiths shrugged. "Doesn't matter much to me."

"I imagine he also skipped town the second you paid him." If he wasn't holed up in a gambling hall nearby, but Nate surmised the man had a little more sense than that.

"Hmm," was all Griffiths said.

Nate didn't know what that meant, but he didn't have long to think on it before Griffiths spoke again.

"He was awfully forthcoming with how cowardly you acted back in the Great Sioux War. Said you near about froze in the middle of a fight. Jumped off your horse and just stood there." Griffiths laughed again and looked at Miss Flagler, as if she might laugh with him. But all she did was shake her head and silently cry.

Nate sucked in a breath. Just the mere mention of the battle he'd never forget sent the horrifying memories flaring across his mind. *Not now*, he tried to tell himself, but it was impossible to push them away. The woman, sobbing over her dead husband. The children, the blood, the fires, and through all of it, gunfire and smoke and horses running and him, just standing there unable to move at the horror of it all. It would always be there. And there was nothing Nate could do to send it away.

He'd always told himself it wasn't cowardice, the way he'd been unable to follow orders that day. But maybe Griffiths and Wallingford were right. He'd been assigned a duty, and he couldn't fulfill it.

It was a betrayal of everything you thought you were. It wasn't what God wanted. That's what he'd always told himself.

"See, he's not right in the head," Griffiths was saying to Miss Flagler, who was watching Nate with the most sorrowful expression. "I believe he did you a favor, turning you away like he did."

Maybe this was what he deserved—to die at the hand of a man like Griffiths. After all, he couldn't bring himself to act when the moment called for it. He couldn't protect himself. He couldn't protect Ruthann.

He was a broken shell of a man.

"I'll give you a choice. You can leave town, or I can put an end to your misery right now," Griffiths said.

"Paul!" Miss Flagler gripped his arm again.

"I'm doing this for *you*," he said.

"This is enough. It isn't what I wanted!" She pulled his arm again, distracting him from Nate.

It was the only opportunity Nate would get to act. He could jump forward, tackle the man to the ground, and wrench the gun away.

But he couldn't do anything. He was too useless, too enmeshed in the past, too . . . cowardly.

"Mr. Harper, please, do something!" Miss Flagler was pleading with him now as Griffiths shoved her aside, shouting that he loved her.

But he still couldn't move.

The door opened again. And this time, Nate knew his world was ending.

Ruthann stood there, her face changing in half a second from one of determination to pure fear—just as Griffiths grabbed hold of her arm and hauled her inside.

Chapter Thirty-one

SHE WAS TOO LATE.

That was Ruthann's only thought as Sissy's beau grabbed her arm and dragged her inside the studio, kicking the door shut behind them with his foot. His fingers dug into her arm as she tried to take in all that was happening.

There was Sissy, pressed against the wall with tears streaming down her face. And then Nate, his arms raised just slightly in front of him with an anguished look upon his face.

"Paul," Sissy sputtered from where she stood.

But the man who held Ruthann paid her no attention.

"You're just in time for your husband's great decision," he said, pulling her against him. "Leave or die, Harper. What will it be?"

But Nate just stood there, that tortured look in his eyes—the one Ruthann recognized. The one that came when he was remembering whatever it was that haunted him from the past. He couldn't have answered the man, not while he was in this state.

But he *had* to, or else . . . Ruthann pushed the thought from her mind. Now was not the time to go to pieces, as easy as that would be. Sissy had already done that as she wailed from her corner, and so it was up to Ruthann to somehow get them out of this situation—alive.

"Nate," she said softly, hoping to stir him from wherever he'd gone in his mind.

"Hush," the man holding her said, and he shook her a little.

Ruthann ignored him. If Paul was focused on her, he couldn't hurt Nate. "Nate!" she said again, louder this time.

"I said—"

"*Nate!*"

Nate blinked. Ruthann barely saw it before Paul had yanked her around to face him. "I told you to stay quiet." He held her in place with one arm, so close she could feel his breath on her face. "I didn't come here intending to hurt you, but if you get in my way, I can't promise you won't be."

Ruthann's stomach clenched, and she instinctively closed her eyes. This all seemed so hopeless. How could she save them all? If only Sissy would rouse herself, or Nate—

All of a sudden, she was flung back as Paul's hand slipped from her arm. Ruthann opened her eyes just before she hit the floor. There, before her, Nate had knocked Paul backward.

She barely felt her own fall. Sissy finally pried herself away from the wall and ran to her side.

"Are you hurt?" she asked.

Ruthann shook her head, barely comprehending Sissy's words or presence as she watched the two men in front of her.

Paul still held the gun as Nate tried to wrestle it away from him. When that didn't work, Nate landed a blow square against the other man's cheek. The impact made Ruthann flinch, but it didn't appear to loosen Paul's grip on the pistol at all.

Nate swung again, but this time Paul blocked the blow with his other arm. At the same time, he raised a knee and managed to push Nate off him.

"You're a coward who can't even fight!" Paul's taunt made Ruthann clench her own fists.

Nate's eyes clouded for just a moment, and he paused.

"Nate!" Ruthann didn't even think before she spoke, but it had been the right choice. The sound of her voice seemed to awaken him, and he pulled himself to his feet as Paul did the same.

Sitting here with Sissy felt useless as the men circled each other. She could run upstairs and attempt to find Nate's guns, the ones she saw him take out only the one time. The other pistol was at her parents' home. She'd packed it in the carpetbag she'd taken when she left the apartment over the studio. But by the time she found and returned with Nate's guns, it might be too late. There had to be something else . . . Something in this studio she could use as a weapon.

She glanced frantically around the room as Paul gave a breathless chuckle and began to raise the gun again. An end table, a lamp, a cushion, a broom— Ruthann leapt to her feet, causing Sissy to give a startled cry.

"Where are you going?" Paul roared as Ruthann ran to the broom. It wouldn't do her much good now that he'd seen her, she thought as her fingers closed around the broom handle. She'd meant to grab it without his notice and somehow sneak up behind him and—

"Ruthann!" Nate's ragged voice tore through her frantic thoughts.

Ruthann spun around, the broom clutched in her hand, only to see Paul pointing the gun at her with fire in his eyes. He didn't hesitate.

A loud roar filled the air—a gunshot—as Sissy screamed.

Nate leapt into the space between Ruthann and Paul, and immediately crumpled to the ground.

"No!" The sound tore from Ruthann's throat. She dropped the broom and ran to Nate, heedless of Paul and his revolver. Out of the corner of her eye, she saw Sissy fly into the man she supposedly loved and begin hitting him with her fists, but the only concern Ruthann had was for Nate.

He was breathing, thankfully. She turned him gently onto his back, and there, on his side, she could see the blood beginning to well up through his shirt and vest.

"No," she said firmly. "No, no, no, no! Do you hear me?"

She was barely conscious of the door opening again, of someone else arriving, of shouts and Sissy crying. Ruthann yanked off the shawl she wore, balled it up, and pressed it to Nate's side.

"Nate," she said, brushing a hand against his face when he opened his eyes. "I'm here."

"I did it," he said, his eyes finding hers.

"You got yourself shot." She didn't know what he was talking about, but she knew people in great pain could go incoherent. Pressing all her strength into staunching his wound with one hand, she grabbed hold of his hand with the other. "Stay awake. Please," she said as he began to close his eyes.

"I did it," he said again, with a slight smile this time. "They didn't win."

"Do you mean Paul? Sissy's beau?" She glanced across the room for the first time since Nate had fallen. One of the sheriff's deputies was placing handcuffs on Paul while the sheriff attempted to calm Sissy.

"I need you to go for the doctor," Sheriff Young was saying to her. He glanced quickly at Nate and Ruthann. "*Now.*"

Sissy finally drew in a great gulp of breath and nodded before running out the door.

"They're getting a doctor," Ruthann said, squeezing Nate's hand as he closed his eyes again. "Nate!"

His eyelids flew open and he smiled as he looked at her. "S-sorry." His voice slurred some, and Ruthann pressed her lips together, trying to keep her fear at bay. It would do him no good if she fell apart now. She had to be strong for him.

"It's all right. Whatever it is, you can tell me later." His eyelids began to close again, and she regretted her words. "Or why don't you tell me now? Nate?"

He smiled again, his eyes half-open. "I love you." The last word was barely a whisper as his eyelids shut.

"Nate. Nate!" Ruthann dropped his hand and gently tapped his cheek, her heart feeling as if it were going to burst out of her chest.

But his eyes didn't open again.

Chapter Thirty-two

WHEN NATE AWOKE, IT was dark. That was odd, because it had been early evening just a moment ago, with the sun not due to set for at least a couple of hours.

He blinked as the room came into focus. This wasn't . . . where was he? He went to sit up in bed, only for a raging pain from his side to take his breath away and cause him to fall back onto the pillow.

"Nate? Are you awake?" Ruthann's sweet, sleepy voice came from somewhere in the room.

Nate forced his eyes open against the pain to find her. And there she was, leaning over him, her face the most welcome sight he could think of seeing upon waking.

"You were shot," she said, answering one of the many questions that spun in his mind. "Are you in pain?"

He nodded.

"Here, just lie back and try not to move. The doctor said it would hurt for a while." She shifted the pillow beneath his head, and Nate smiled up at her gratefully.

"You're at my parents' house. Stuart kindly offered his room." She arranged herself in a chair that someone must have placed by the bedside.

Nate let his eyes travel the shadowy room that now looked familiar. How many hours had he whiled away in this house with Stuart when they were young? He decided it was good to be in a place of happy memories when one was in such pain.

He'd been shot . . .

"Do you remember what happened?" Ruthann asked.

It was beginning to come together, fuzzy at first, but the more he followed the paths his mind laid out, the more he remembered.

"Miss Flagler came to see me. To warn me. And her fiancé . . . Griffiths is his name. He arrived with the pistol. And then you were there and—" He stopped speaking. Had he really done what his mind was telling him he did?

"You saved my life," Ruthann said in a whisper.

Nate swallowed, his throat as dry as the scrubby hills outside of town in the fall.

"Here." Ruthann held a glass of water out, and Nate raised his head just far enough to take a sip.

As the cool liquid eased his parched throat, it seemed to clear his head too.

He *had* jumped in front of Ruthann. He'd acted. He'd protected her when the time came.

"Do you want more?" She held the glass out again, and he shook his head, still marveling at how quickly things had changed.

"I didn't think I could do that," he finally said.

Ruthann looked up from the glass she'd set on the night table. "But you did." She paused, placing her hands in her lap and chewing her lip. "Will you tell me? What it is that haunts you so? I know it must be terrible, but I can hear it, Nate. I'm strong enough. I can listen, and I promise nothing you can say will shock me or make me change my mind about you."

He traced the fine features of her face with his eyes. She was so beautiful, so perfect, so fragile—no. She wasn't fragile at all, and she'd proven that, time and again. He almost winced as he thought of the things he'd said to her to make her leave. And yet here she was, at his side, despite all of that.

It was almost as if she knew why he'd said those words.

"I'm sorry for hurting you," he said. "I want you to know that. And I suppose you know this already, but I meant none of it. I thought I was being noble."

She nodded, but didn't say anything.

She was waiting for more.

And in that moment, he knew she deserved honesty. He needn't describe every detail, but she ought to know what had happened, and why he couldn't ever seem to leave it behind.

He drew in a breath and told himself they were only memories. "It happened not long after I went to the Dakota Territory, about a year after I enlisted." And so he told her, of the Great Sioux War, of the singular battle north of the Black Hills that had shaken every moral fiber of his being to its core, of how he'd been unable to move upon seeing the inhumanity that men he'd come to think of as friends had enacted upon one little village, of how he'd done nothing but stood fixed in one place, and of how the vivid memories had taken up residence in his mind ever since.

Afterward, Ruthann slid from the chair to the edge of the bed, and gently, she'd laid her head and a hand on his chest. Nate rested one of his hands on the back of her head and let a breath of relief shudder through him as he closed his eyes.

How was it that the simple telling of a horrible tale made him feel as if he'd been born anew? It was as if he could breathe freely again. The memories were still there—he was certain they'd never disappear—but they were in the past.

"You were never a coward," Ruthann said, her voice thrumming through him straight to his heart. "You were simply a good man. And you still are. Thank you for telling me."

He let her words sink in. He had *acted* when it came to saving Ruthann. He hadn't been a coward when it counted. And . . . he let her words tumble through his mind . . . She was right.

He tightened his hold around her and breathed in her scent. "I am so sorry," he said again. He didn't think he could ever apologize enough. She'd done nothing but be her true, kind, incredible self, and he'd tossed that aside.

"I forgive you," she said, lifting her head to catch his eyes. "Do you forgive yourself?"

"Maybe not yet. Not for how I treated you. But I'll work on it."

She smiled. "I suppose that's all I can ask. Now . . . I don't suppose you remember what you said right before you lost consciousness?"

He wrinkled his forehead in jest. He did, in fact, remember. "I imagine I asked if the hardware store had ordered new glass for the back door?"

Ruthann's eyebrows twitched down, confused, but only for a second. Then she gave him a sly grin. "Oh, I told Mr. Yost that he needn't order any. You much preferred the look of a torn burlap sack over a glass window."

Nate started to laugh, which immediately made a dose of fiery pain course through his side.

Ruthann slapped a hand over her mouth. "Oh, no, I'm sorry! Are you all right?"

Nate grimaced but hid it quickly with a smile. "I'll be fine. Just don't make me laugh. These are serious times."

That drew a grin from her again. "You do remember, don't you?"

He opened his hand, waiting for hers, and she granted his request. As he wrapped her fingers securely in his, he nodded. "I'm fairly certain I told you I love you."

She beamed, and Nate didn't think he'd ever seen anything prettier in his life.

"The usual thing to do is to say the same to the man who says it to you," he supplied.

Ruthann blushed. "Nate Harper, I do believe you're acting as you did when you were nineteen."

He did feel younger, almost as if he weren't carrying a weight the size of a mountain on his back.

"I hope to tease you often, but I'm afraid I can't do that if you don't feel about me the same as I feel for you." He raised his eyebrows in mock indignation.

Ruthann shook her head. "I love you. You know I do. I just as much as told you so that evening in front of the fire."

"I don't know if I believe it without a kiss," he said, shrugging the shoulder on the side that didn't hurt.

"You are incorrigible. But yes, I love you. And yes, I'll kiss you." She leaned over him then and pressed her lips to his.

Nate laid his free hand against the back of her head, relishing the feel of her mouth against his. She sighed, and he decided it was a good thing he was incapacitated, or he'd be tempted to pull her down beside him.

She drew away slightly, out of breath, and he tangled his hand in her hair, hoping to convince her to come back, to kiss him until neither of them could breathe.

"I don't suppose you'll want to stay Mrs. Harper after that?" he said.

She laughed, and before he knew it, she was kissing him again, her hand clutching his shoulder.

He would never let her go, not again. Ruthann knew him through and through, and he would keep her safe until his last days.

With her, he was brave enough to face anything.

Epilogue

THE FOLLOWING SUMMER . . .

Ruthann had to pause to catch her breath. Tommy Robinson and his sister Anna turned around and fell into a fit of giggles when they saw her, leaning against a tree, sweating, and resting a hand on her enormous belly.

"Go on," Ruthann called to them. "I'll never keep up with you two."

The children laughed again, ran back to give her a big hug around each leg, and then tore off down the hill and through the crowd that had gathered for the town picnic.

Ruthann leaned her back against the tree, relishing the small bit of shade it gave on the hot day. The baby was due to arrive in less than a month, and not a day passed lately that she didn't wish it might decide to come just a little bit early.

This was the perfect vantage point, just high enough to see half the town spread out before her, along the banks of the river. A handful of men had gathered a small band and were playing a lively tune. There was dancing, and games, and a few men were even racing horses, down past the edge of town and back again.

And there was food, of course. More food than Ruthann had ever thought to see in her life. The women in town had cooked up every chicken and potato and vegetable that could be found, and it was all laid out in a long spread with a pretty mismatch of tablecloths fluttering in the occasional, very welcome breeze.

Ruthann continued searching the crowd for one person in particular. She waved to Grace Hill and her sister-in-law Molly, who sat with their babies near the water. Just beyond, Sissy Flagler—still unmarried but no longer in much of a hurry to wed—chatted with several other women. She'd become much more tolerable, and almost friendly, since her fiancé had found himself locked up in the Territorial Prison. She'd even brought Ruthann a set of hairpins she claimed to have ordered straight from New York as a belated wedding gift.

Penny Young, the sheriff's wife, presided over the food tables. Ruthann could think of no one better for the job, save for her own mother, but Mama was far too busy trying to find the "perfect man"—as she'd put it—for Norah. It seemed that seeing Ruthann so happy had then caused Mama much distress over Norah's unmarried state. She spotted them both now, poor Norah roped into conversation with some hapless gentleman while Mama looked on, eagerly hoping for a love match.

Ruthann frowned as she reached the end of the crowd and still didn't see Nate. He shouldn't be that difficult to find with his photography equipment. The mayor had put him in charge of commemorating the big moments of the event, and Nate took the job seriously, setting up hours ago, before anyone had arrived for the picnic.

"There you are."

Ruthann turned at the sound of the voice she wanted to hear the most. Nate stood behind her, holding his hat as he drew the back of his hand across his forehead.

"I was looking for you," she said. "How is it going?"

"Very well. I've captured images of the band, of Francis Stiller's winning horse, and of Mrs. Young and all of that food. The mayor is supposed to give a speech in thirty minutes, so I have time until then." Nate looked pleased with himself, and that made Ruthann well up with pride.

"I hope none of the other photographers were too angry at not having been chosen," she said.

Nate waved his hand. "They're fine. Old Man Thomas is on the verge of closing up shop anyhow, and Garth was hoping to spend the day with his family."

Ruthann nodded. The baby kicked just then, and she grabbed hold of Nate's hand and rested it against her. "I think he likes the music," she said.

"Or the sound of his—or her—father's voice," Nate replied. He smiled almost reverently at her stomach. "I can't believe we'll be meeting this little person soon. It's nothing short of a miracle."

"That it is," Ruthann said. "Although I believe it will be an even greater miracle when I can walk without coming up short of breath again."

"Well, I think you look beautiful just like this." Nate wrapped his arms around her, and she leaned gratefully into his embrace. "Perhaps we should have another baby immediately after this one is born."

She gave him a look she hoped indicated that he'd taken leave of his senses.

"All right, maybe not *immediately*," he said with a laugh.

Seeing him so happy never failed to amaze her, and Ruthann laughed too. He still had moments now and then when she'd catch him looking as if he were somewhere else, and he continued to avoid touching a pistol unless it was absolutely needed. But he was Nate again—the Nate she'd always known and had loved. Lively, sweet, and teasing, but with an older and more assured weight to his personality.

"I love you," she said, those thoughts still swirling about her mind. "I don't think I could ever love anyone as much as I love you."

"Just wait until that baby is born," he said, trying but failing to keep the teasing grin from his face. "I'll be second best at that point."

"You'll be no such thing. There is no 'second best' in our home. Now, will you kiss me before you run off to photograph the mayor?"

And Nate complied, drawing her to him as best he could. Ruthann sighed into the kiss. It would never get old, this feeling of losing herself entirely in him. Every day, for the rest of her life, she would yearn for this feeling, for him.

He was, quite simply, the love of her life, and she thrilled at the thought of spending the rest of her years with him and their growing family. Through births and seasons and passing time, their love would grow.

And she couldn't wait to experience every moment of it.

THANK YOU SO MUCH FOR reading! I hope you enjoyed Ruthann and Nate's story. And don't worry, Norah gets her own story next! While searching for a way to help her brother, Norah finds help—and possibly love—with a character you've already met. Can you figure out who it is? Check out the <u>pre-order for *Norah* to find out if you're right</u>[1]!

Want to read more of my sweet historical western books? A good place to start is with *Building Forever*[2], the first book in my Gilbert Girls series. This series is where you'll find out how Cañon City's Sheriff Ben Young and his wife Penny first met.

To be alerted about my new books, sign up here: http://bit.ly/catsnewsletter I give subscribers a free download of *Forbidden Forever*, a prequel novella to my Gilbert Girls series. You'll also get sneak peeks at upcoming books, insights into the writer life, discounts and deals, inspirations, and so much more. I'd love to have *you* join the fun!

Turn the page to see a complete list of my books, including all the books in the Brides of Fremont County series.

---

1. https://amzn.to/3IyJRuA

2.   *http://bit.ly/BuildingForeverbook*

More Books by Cat Cahill

***Crest Stone Mail-Order Brides* series**
A Hopeful Bride[1]
A Rancher's Bride[2]
A Bartered Bride[3]
***The Gilbert Girls* series**
Building Forever[4]
Running From Forever[5]
Wild Forever[6]
Hidden Forever[7]
Forever Christmas[8]
On the Edge of Forever[9]
The Gilbert Girls Book Collection – Books 1-3[10]
The Gilbert Girls Book Collection – Books 4-6[11]

1. https://bit.ly/HopefulBride

2. http://bit.ly/RanchersBride

3. https://bit.ly/barteredbride

4. http://bit.ly/BuildingForeverbook

5. http://bit.ly/RunningForeverBook

6. http://bit.ly/WildForeverBook

7. http://bit.ly/HiddenForeverBook

8. http://bit.ly/ForeverChristmasBook

9. http://bit.ly/EdgeofForever

10. http://bit.ly/GilbertGirlsBox

Brides of Fremont County series
Grace[12]
Molly[13]
Ruthann[14]
Norah[15]
Charlotte (part of the Secrets, Scandals, & Seduction boxset)[16]

Other Sweet Historical Western Romances by Cat

The Proxy Brides series
A Bride for Isaac [17]
A Bride for Andrew [18]
A Bride for Weston[19]

The Blizzard Brides series
A Groom for Celia [20]
A Groom for Faith[21]
A Groom for Josie[22]

Last Chance Brides series
A Chance for Lara[23]

---

11. https://amzn.to/3gYPXcA

12. http://bit.ly/ConfusedColorado

13. https://bit.ly/DejectedDenver

14. https://bit.ly/brideruthann

15. https://amzn.to/3IyJRuA

16. https://books2read.com/u/4joPNj

17. http://bit.ly/BrideforIsaac

18. https://bit.ly/BrideforAndrew

19. https://bit.ly/BrideforWeston

20. http://bit.ly/GroomforCelia

21. http://bit.ly/GroomforFaith

22. https://bit.ly/GroomforJosie

The Matchmaker's Ball series
Waltzing with Willa[24]
Westward Home and Hearts Mail-Order Brides series
Rose's Rescue[25]
Matchmaker's Mix-Up series
William's Wistful Bride[26]
Ransom's Rowdy Bride[27]
The Sheriff's Mail-Order Bride series
A Bride for Hawk[28]
Keepers of the Light series
The Outlaw's Promise[29]
Mail-Order Brides' First Christmas series
A Christmas Carol for Catherine[30]
The Broad Street Boarding House series
Starla's Search[31]

23. https://amzn.to/3sAj0IV

24. https://bit.ly/WaltzingwithWilla

25. https://bit.ly/RoseRescue

26. https://bit.ly/WilliamsWistfulBride

27. https://amzn.to/3s0Lqwq

28. https://bit.ly/BrideforHawk

29. https://bit.ly/OutlawsPromise

30. https://bit.ly/ChristmasCarolCatherine

31. https://amzn.to/32sQuPS

About the Author, Cat Cahill

A SUNSET. SNOW ON THE mountains. A roaring river in the spring. A man and a woman who can't fight the love that pulls them together. The danger and uncertainty of life in the Old West. This is what inspires me to write. I hope you find an escape in my books!

I live with my family and a houseful of dogs and cats in Kentucky. When I'm not writing, I'm losing myself in a good book, planning my next travel adventure, doing a puzzle, attempting to garden, or wrangling my kids.

Made in United States
Troutdale, OR
08/05/2023

11837658R00127